MARCO

LUCIAN & LIA: BOOK 8

SYDNEY LANDON

1

Marco

I sit in my car outside Nina Gavino's apartment as I've done often in the past year. Only this time, things are different. Unrest akin to panic exists in the Gavino organization, and it's no longer safe for Nina to be on her own. I have been fixated on the beautiful little minx since she quite literally rescued me from a pile of dog shit after I was poisoned. I've pursued her to no avail. She wants nothing to do with the mafia... or me. She had enough of that as the stepdaughter of the recently deceased Franklin Gavino—head of the Gavino family. And considering I am the son of the head of the Moretti family, I'm completely entangled in the life she's so determined to avoid.

But none of that matters any longer. Franklin and his son, Frankie Jr. were killed last night, and now no one is safe or above suspicion. The Morettis might be allies of the Gavinos, but my word alone will not stop them from harming Nina should they decide to. And thanks to Frankie Jr.'s obsession with his stepsister, many in the organization know her name all too well.

The only way I can ensure her safety is to have her under my protection. And that's exactly what I intend to do. It's a drastic step to take for someone who is essentially a stranger. Especially one who avoids me like the fucking plague. *Why*, you might ask, would I do something like this for her when there are so many willing women out there? *Because* I want her more than I've ever wanted another woman. And... I feel responsible for her predicament. After all, I killed Franklin and his son.

Wait, did I forget to mention that rather pertinent fact?

Possibly, I should have led with it. But being mafia means that I've never been one to freely share information, especially the type that could get me and a shitload of people I care about killed. Or "deaded" as Lee Jacks's son, Victor, calls it. That kid cracks me up. Personally, I also like that he's calling everyone a "fucker" now, but we're under strict orders from the Wrenn women not to laugh about it. He's two, says *fuck-errr* with the cutest bad-toddler face, and attempts to wink at the same time. Who could not laugh at that? And why must Nic and I listen to—and obey—the Wrenn women even though Lee and Tony are the ones who married Jade and Jacey? *Fucking family.*

I know I'm deliberately taking a trip down memory lane to postpone the inevitable confrontation with Nina. There's no way she'll meekly pack her bags and come with me. Abducting her would be less painful than enduring the tongue-lashing I'll receive. *Why does something that sounds so naughty make my balls sweat—in trepidation?* Fuck it all, I'm Marco Moretti. I'm feared by men who'd kill their own mother without hesitation. I've seen and done more in my thirty-seven years than most will in a lifetime—if they're lucky. I'm an enforcer for the Moretti family, but not the type you see in movies. I'm no low-life thug who gets his kicks by breaking fingers when someone can't repay their loan. That shit is old school. Sure, some gangs do that very thing, but not the Morettis. We've evolved and have varied and complex holdings all over the world. And like Lee and Tony, much of those are legal—or close enough to escape detection by the authorities. Those legit businesses launder vast amounts of money through our organization. Nic and I jokingly refer to ourselves as dry cleaners because, in a sense, that's exactly what we oversee for the family. Up until last night, the Gavinos had been one of our biggest customers. But with the death of their leader, chaos has ensued, and until they get their shit together and someone steps forward to take charge, the Morettis can no longer risk being financially linked with them. The police in Asheville, North Carolina, might be able to look the other way at times where we're concerned, but there is too much noise on the streets right now for them to ignore the situation should it continue to escalate. And I sure as fuck don't intend to stand around with my dick in one hand and a guilty sign in the other.

I'm still sitting in my BMW X6 when my cell phone rings. I glance down and see Nic's name. Nicoli Moretti is my cousin a few times removed and my best friend. He's also one of the few people brave enough to give me hell, which he does without preamble when I connect the call. "You chicken shit."

I don't often play dumb, but now seems like a good time to try. "What're you talking about, asshole?" *Yeah, that even sounds weak to my own ears.*

"I'm speaking of the fact that you've yet to speak to Nina, much less encourage her to be your lady friend."

"My *lady friend*? Have you been reading those historical chick books again? No one says stuff like that anymore, man. I'm embarrassed for you."

Instead of sounding offended, I literally hear the amusement dripping from his voice when he says, "Be that as it may, bro, it doesn't change the fact that you need to grow a pair and handle this. Otherwise, walk away and let it be. There's a chance the Gavinos won't even look her way, so this could all be for nothing."

"That's a risk I'm not willing to take—considering. And for your information, I'm waiting for her to pack right now. Bet you feel pretty fucking stupid for your assumptions." *That's better.*

The other line is silent for a moment before Nic laughs—*the bastard actually laughs.* "You know, I might have bought into that if I hadn't been sitting across the street from you for half an hour now, fucker. And the fact you haven't noticed a vehicle as big as the Escalade is just sad, man—fucking tragic. You're slipping in your old age. And it also needs to be said that you're becoming a bit of a pussy. That girl weighs what, one hundred pounds soaking wet? What's she gonna do, attack your damn ankles?"

Fuck my life. Absolutely, fuck it. "I swear if you mention this to Tony or Lee, I'll shoot you," I mutter wryly.

"Why bother?" he asks sarcastically. "They're as henpecked as you are. Swear to Christ, the great Anthony Moretti has even admitted to buying tampons for Jacey at Walgreens. I'm the only real man left around here."

"Shut the fuck up," I grumble as I glare in his direction. He's right; the Escalade is the size of a bus. Certainly not easy to overlook, especially when you're usually innately astute and notice something as small as an ant creeping by. With no more words, I disconnect the call and release a breath of frustration before opening my door and stepping onto the sidewalk. I don't bother to survey the area at this point. Nic will have already done that several times over while I've been hiding in my car. I walk toward Nina's apartment on legs that are unusually heavy. *This is fucking absurd.* Nic's right; why am I letting this get to me so badly? *Fear of rejection? Guilt?* Yeah, the list is endless and varied, but now isn't the time for this kind of self-reflection. *I'll save that for Dr. Phil.*

I raise my hand to press the buzzer and take a step back in surprise when the door suddenly opens to reveal a scowling Nina. *Don't let her see you sweat. Be cool.* "What are you doing here, Moretti?" she asks crossly. A grin tugs at my lips as she puts her hands on her hips and glares at me. *This is probably the way King Kong felt when he was making goo-goo eyes at his pint-sized soul mate.*

I put my hands on top of the door frame and let my eyes wander leisurely down her small body. *Dear God, she has those granny glasses on the strap around her neck again. So fucking hot.* Her dark hair is in a sloppy bun, and she's wearing a short dress with one corner hanging off her shoulder. Her feet are bare, and each of her toenails is painted a different color, something that suits her quirky personality very well. My gaze returns to meet hers as I give a nod of approval. "Miss me?"

She blinks up at me a few times in surprise before sputtering out, "Miss you? Hardly. It's obviously the other way around since you've once again chosen to show up unannounced. Don't you have some thug friends to hang out with?"

I wiggle my brow suggestively. "There are many people who would more than enjoy my company... in a variety of ways."

"You're a pig." She scoffs, rolling her eyes in disgust. Then she has the audacity to make a shooing motion with her hands. "Please don't let me keep you from banging some airhead. Maybe you'll find one who can count to five without using her fingers."

I can't help it; I laugh as I always do when she starts tossing out insults. I've never had a woman talk so much shit to my face. Granted, there have been a few haters through the years, but I usually try not to burn bridges—especially ones I might want to cross again. I click my tongue in a move that is meant to irritate the hell out of her. "Jealousy suits you, Belle. You're even sexier when you're all fired up. Don't worry, though; you're still in the running for the top position if you play your cards right."

She's choking in indignation now, and I'm kind of afraid she's going to pull out the gun she usually carries and shoot my dick off. She attempts to shut the door in my face, but I wedge my foot inside at the last moment. For such a tiny thing, she's surprisingly strong. Thank fuck I'm wearing boots or I'd be limping for a month. "Of all the nicknames you could have picked, why Belle? You know what, never mind? You probably call your women that because you cycle through them too quickly to know their actual names. "Now, could you please go away? I have a deadline approaching, and I need to get back to work. Find someone else to stroke your ego because it's not happening here, Romeo."

"Fortunately, I don't need that from you or any other woman," I say honestly. It's not that I think I'm that handsome; it's simply that I don't give a fuck about anyone's opinion. *Except hers.* I ignore the annoying voice in my head as I get to the business at hand. "You need to pack a bag so we can get out of here. I have no idea if you're at risk, but it's safer at this point to assume you are."

She opens her mouth, then closes it again before rubbing one of her temples. "Is it too much to ask that you speak in coherent sentences, Moretti? It's getting late, and I don't want to play the guessing game with you."

It strikes me as ironic that I'm lecturing her on safety while standing in her doorway with no one watching my back. *Might as well be wearing a bull's-eye.* Of course, it's highly unlikely that anything would escape Nic's attention. Unlike me, he's not distracted by a woman. It's downright scary how much of my mafia training has gone down the drain in the past hour alone. If the Gavinos wanted me, they'd have easily taken me out tonight. And that's a sobering thought. Without asking for permission, I push her gently backward a few feet and close the door behind us. *Is she growling at me? Mmm.* "Until we know what will happen with Franklin and Frankie gone, you need to go to ground. You can do that at my place for now. I'll have someone cover you when I'm not there." The confusion in her eyes tells me something that should have occurred to me given her distant relationship with her stepfather. I assumed that Minka Gavino—her best friend—would have gotten word to her by now. *Fuck.*

"What are you talking about?" she asks uncertainly.

I've always been a man who believes in ripping the Band-Aid off quickly, so I do exactly that. "You haven't heard that Franklin and Frankie were killed last night?" And there it is, the shocked expression that confirms what I suspected—she had no idea.

"I—no." She shakes her head in denial. "Franklin sent word just last week that he was going to be out of town for a while on business. And Frankie almost always accompanies him. I'm sure if you contacted one of his lieutenants, they'd tell you that." She lets out a shaky laugh. "Really, Moretti, aren't you a bit too gangster to be making assumptions?"

I gently place a hand on each of her slim shoulders as if bracing her for my words. "There's no mistake. I saw their bodies with my own eyes. They're dead. That's not something we'd ever accept as truth without proof." *She's going down,* I think a split second later as her eyes roll back into her head and she goes limp in my hold. As strong as I am, I still barely keep her from hitting the floor. Dead weight is hard to deal with even when the person is as light as Nina. "Fuck," I bite out as I awkwardly lift her into my arms and carry her to the sofa—the same one I spent time on after Nina rescued me from the nearby woods. Of course, getting poisoned will turn most any day to shit in a hurry. Factor in all the barfing and feeling like you're going to die, and yeah, it sucked. But it brought Nina into my life, and for that, I'm almost thankful. Unwilling to let the chance to hold her pass, I sit and attempt to arrange her comfortably against my chest. By this point, she's already stirring, and I know this moment of closeness is almost over. In truth, clinging to her while she's unconscious is probably a bit like rifling through a woman's underwear drawer, but I guess that's what I've been reduced to.

"Wh—what," she murmurs as she shifts restlessly.

"Shh, I've got you," I whisper reassuringly. "Don't make any sudden movements unless you want to end up on your back." *That definitely sounded better in my head.*

"What in the hell?" she hisses out as she pushes against my hold. I don't detect any real anger, though, just confusion. *Join the club, sweetheart.*

I attempt to maintain my gentle tone to avoid startling her further. "You passed out. I was going to lay you down, but you were stuck to me like glue. Never would have figured you for one of those chicks who try to take advantage of a gentleman."

I'm relieved to see the bloom of color in her face, even if it's caused by anger. She was entirely too pale a few moments ago. "I don't know how you managed to get me in this position, Moretti, but there is no way—oh, shit." She's mid-tirade when it hits her. I see her eyes widen and fill with moisture as her words trail off. I wait, wanting to make sure I'm not reading her wrong. She blinks a few times, then her eyes lock on mine. The vulnerability I see there has me catching my breath. "He's really gone, isn't he? You wouldn't tell me that unless you were positive." The last part is a statement and not a question, but I nod once anyway. "How?" she asks as she stares off into the distance.

"Does it really matter? The result is the same."

She's pissed again now, and it's a hell of a lot easier to handle than her sorrow. "Don't be a wimp. You came over here to deliver the news, so don't start withholding information now."

"Gunshot to the forehead," I state bluntly.

Her brows furrow, and then she moves until she's straddling me. We're face to face with only inches separating our mouths. I don't think she realizes the intimacy of the position, but my cock certainly does. *Down, boy. So not the time.* "That's not right, is it? Aren't mafia hits usually to the back of the head? You know, execution style?"

Fuck. I run a hand through my hair, attempting to gather my thoughts. "That's just in the movies or on television. Real life is seldom so scripted. Hypothetically, even if a murder were planned, I'd say it seldom plays out in that exact fashion. Anytime multiple people are involved, there's no way to predict an outcome." *That's putting it mildly.*

She looks thoughtful now as she mulls over my explanation. "I see your point. What you mean is Franklin likely wouldn't have accepted his fate without a fight. So the killer would be forced to take whatever shot he could, even if it was messy. I'd say we're probably talking about an amateur here. That should narrow things down, right?"

Messy? An amateur? Say what? Years of training keeps my face impassive even though she's trampled upon a few nerves. "I hardly think we can deduce anything from the location of the bullet, other than the fact that the killer is obviously an excellent marksman. Have you any idea how difficult that kind of shot would be?"

Before I can stop her, she flops backward out of my hold and onto the sofa beside me. *Where did her ninja moves come from?* She crosses her arms and turns up her small nose. "Gee, I hope we find him soon so you can join his fan club. Maybe you can form your own crime ring together." I open my mouth, then close it again as she snaps her fingers loudly. "Oh wait, you're already a member of the mob, and I'm betting it's not like some online Facebook group where you're allowed to join as many as you want. And you sure can't leave without ending up swimming with the fishes. There's always the secret admirer route. Do you even do social media? Facebook? Twitter? Instagram? Snapchat? Pinterest?"

How in the hell can she talk this fast without stopping to draw a breath?

Fuck me. At least I know how women achieve their twenty thousand words-per-day quotas. They just don't breathe as often as men. "What the fuck is Pinterest?" I ask absently as I try to digest all the shit she's tossed out. Somehow, I think my question lowers her opinion of me even further, if possible.

"You really need to get with it, Moretti. There is this whole world outside of your gang. Even prisoners use social media to find romance."

"So you're saying Pinterest is a dating site?" I give her a cocky grin that has her visibly gritting her teeth. "Trust me, baby, I don't need any help in that area."

"As all the STDs you've acquired would attest to." I fight the urge to cover my crotch when she adds, "I don't care what they say, I believe your dick can certainly fall off from diseases and overuse."

How's it possible to be both offended and turned on? This is some seriously fucked-up shit. In the space of moments, I had the two things I'm most proud of insulted: my shooting abilities and my cock. *Although, probably not in that order...* How much can a man be expected to endure in one sitting? Without thinking, I grumble, "What does my sex life have to do with Franklin's death? You're all over the place, Belle. If you haven't been checked for ADHD, I highly recommend it."

I could kick myself when her face falls as reality comes crashing back in. Why hadn't I kept my mouth shut and let her continue? Was my ego really that fragile? *Um, yeah.* "I—how could I have forgotten that? I said all that silly stuff." She appears to be studying her hands intently now as she whispers huskily, "It's not as if I had any kind of real relationship with him, no matter how much he tried. Don't get me wrong. I know he isn't—I mean, he wasn't a good man. But he was decent to my mom while she was alive and did everything he could for her when she got sick. She adored him, and I believe he felt the same. She sold her soul for that love—but I never did. I got out as soon as I could. If not for promising my mom, he'd never have let me make a life of my own."

I shrug my shoulders, not bothering to confirm or deny her statement. Undoubtedly, she's right, but it matters little now. "Franklin was one of the few decent men left."

"Honor among thieves." She snorts. "I lived with him and his spawn for several years, so you don't have to try to make him into something he wasn't for my benefit." A shiver passes through her small frame when she adds, "And Frankie Jr. would have been the devil himself if he'd been smart enough to pull it off. The people in this city better be grateful he was a few sandwiches short of a picnic. Otherwise, he'd have been unstoppable."

"Frankie was... challenged." I nod thoughtfully. I've never made a secret of my disdain for the other man, and I won't pretend otherwise. *That would certainly look suspicious to the wrong people.* "I often thought Franklin would have been relieved had Frankie been taken out. He'd have avenged him, of course, but then he'd have moved on and damn sure lived a more peaceful existence. Regardless of what you think, business is business, and when you have a loose link, they pull everyone else down with them. But being family makes it tricky."

"Then it doubly sucks that Franklin didn't live to enjoy his son's demise," she murmurs. I fight the urge to squirm when she stares at me intently. "Do you have any idea who did it? The Morettis run Asheville, don't they? Surely, something this big couldn't happen without you guys getting wind of it."

Fuck, she's a danger to herself. She needs to understand there could be dire consequences should the wrong person hear her. "Nina, you cannot say that shit. Hell, don't even think it." There are no traces of humor in my voice now. "You're already in a vulnerable position with your connection to Franklin. Don't act as if you have any knowledge of the inner workings of the Morettis or Gavinos. Everyone is under intense scrutiny now, and you must think carefully before you speak."

As much as I hate scaring her, I'm relieved to see that my words have the desired effect. She's clearly unnerved—and that could save her life. "There's no reason for anyone to look twice at me, Marco. I haven't seen anyone but Minka in months."

I lay my head back on the sofa for a moment as fatigue threatens to overtake me. It's been a long few days, and I'm so beyond tired at this point. "Your friendship with Minka is not a plus. You can be damn sure that her father keeps an eye on her, so everyone in the Gavino family knows that not only are you tied to Franklin and his idiot son, but also to Raymond's daughter. Which wouldn't be a big deal if you were family. But you're a well-connected outsider, and that is dangerous."

"But what about Tony and Lee?" she asks defensively. "They're Moretti royalty, yet they've distanced themselves without issues."

My jaw snaps shut in frustration as I glare at her. "Did I not just fucking tell you to stop speaking as if you're an expert on things you shouldn't be? I swear to God, I hope you and your friend don't talk about shit like this is public." I reach out and put my hand on her arm, hoping she can feel the gravity of her situation. "Your best friend is Minka Gavino. Her father is now likely the head of the family. Minka's activities will be monitored more closely. I'm well aware of your disdain for our... way of life, but it's imperative you keep those opinions to yourself. It would be wise to avoid Minka altogether, but that's probably not going to happen. So when you do see her, stick to safe topics."

"Like shopping and boys?" she says, sounding like one of the bimbos she accuses me of favoring.

I pretend not to notice her sarcasm. "Exactly, Belle."

She wrinkles her nose in the adorable way I find so sexy. "We're not stupid. We've had our own language for years, Moretti. Don't you think we're aware that some nosy asshole might be getting his rocks off by listening to us? Believe it or not, women are capable of more than lying on their backs and bending over."

That last part has my blood pressure spiking. I resist the urge to adjust, afraid she'll pull her gun out from wherever she has it stashed. I clear my throat as I try to clear the image of her bent over the damn sofa we're sitting on from my head. "Er... could you be a bit more specific? If you two are speaking a foreign language, I'm pretty sure they can have it translated."

Shaking her head in amusement, she says, "That's not it. We invented our own. And don't bother to ask any more questions because I'm not telling you. That would kind of defeat the purpose, wouldn't it? For all I know, you're wearing a wire. You said to trust no one, and I have to assume you were including yourself in that."

Baby, you have no idea. I want to continue this debate because I get off on these crazy arguments, but I've already been here too long. I've barely processed that thought when her doorbell sounds. We both jump, which I'm grateful no one is here to witness. *She's going to be the death of me.* She's off the sofa and halfway across the room before I reach her. "What in the hell are you doing? Have you heard nothing I said?"

When I attempt to move past her, the little hellion elbows me in the side. "Ouch," I hiss. The jab was surprisingly strong coming from someone so petite. She mumbles a word under her breath that has me narrowing my eyes. *Surely, I heard that wrong.* "What did you say?"

If I expect her to back down, I'm sorely mistaken. She straightens her spine and puts her hands on her hips. "I said you're such a pussy." As I'm choking on my indignation, she slips around me and opens the door. I pull the gun from my ankle holster and aim over her shoulder. "Oh great, good cop is here. And I was afraid I'd be stuck with just the asshole one this time. Lucky me."

Nic chuckles as he pulls Nina into a side hug that lasts a little longer than necessary. Come to think of it, they're not buddies, so why is physical contact necessary at all? And she's calmly allowing the embrace. She'd have her knee in my crotch by now. *I'm far too fixated on her doing bad things to my dick.* "How's life treating you, Rambo?" He chuckles affectionately, and I'm further annoyed to see her lips twitch in amusement.

She inclines her head in my direction, all hints of laughter gone. "It was fine until your buddy hiked up his leg and pissed all over my day. Not only has he told me that Franklin and Frankie are dead, but he also has some insane notion that I'll pack a bag and go along with him docilely, like one of his bimbos."

Nic winces at me, then dares to stroll past us and sprawl out on the sofa. Nina follows, not appearing bothered by it in the least. I almost expect her to stretch out next to him, but luckily, that doesn't happen. Instead, she perches on the edge of a nearby chair as if waiting for something. Nic reaches out and picks up a magazine off the coffee table and begins thumbing through it. Without looking up, he says, "Seems like you're having a tough time here, bro. I gathered that must be the case when an hour passed and there was no sign of you."

"I couldn't just blurt it out," I snap defensively.

"Really?" Nina laughs. "You plowed through the news like a bull in a china shop. If that was your attempt at breaking it to me gently, then your technique needs work."

I open my mouth to deliver a sarcastic retort but close it again abruptly when I notice the way her hands tremble as she clasps them together in her lap. I see her blinking back tears as she stares off in the distance. It's something I often do when I'm attempting to gather my composure. Although, in my case, it's usually to deal with anger and not grief. Regardless of her relationship with Franklin, I shouldn't expect her grief to be so short-lived. Naturally, as soon as her mind isn't occupied by other thoughts, she'll feel the loss again. *If she ever discovers what I've done, I'll be as dead to her as Franklin is.* Nic also notices the shift in her mood and attempts to fill the silence. "It's a guy thing," he says simply.

When I see her eyes narrow, I know he's accomplished his objective of distracting her. "So, since you have a penis, you're not bound by the usual laws of human decency?" Before he can respond, she slaps her hand on her forehead. "Oh, excuse me, I forgot who I'm dealing with. Laws don't apply to your kind."

"*Our kind*," Nic mimics.

"You're getting kinda mean in your old age, Rambo. What are you, like forty now?" He nods as if that explains it all. I don't bother to point out that we're closer to the big four-oh than she is.

"Are you going through 'the change?' My mother blames everything on that. I swear she's scarier than an assassin with a machine gun."

I fully expect her to lose her shit. What woman likes to be called menopausal, especially when she's only thirty-five. But she merely picks up a coaster and chucks it at him. She grins when it bounces off his chest, and he pretends to be injured. *What the fuck?* How is it that Nic can get away with anything, whereas I get my ass chewed out for commenting on the weather? "If you two are finished, we need to get out of here." I see by the stubborn set of her mouth that she's digging in her heels for a lengthy argument. And there isn't time for it. Nic's right; we've already been here too long. I know I'll hate myself, but I do it anyway. "Unless you want to end up with a bullet in your head like Franklin, you'll pack a bag—now. This isn't an order, Nina, but it *is* a one-time offer. If you want to be safe until we know what we're dealing with, then you'll come with me. If you're confident in your abilities to handle whatever shit the Gavinos may possibly toss your way, then stay here." I glance at my watch. "You have five minutes before we leave, with or without you."

Her eyes are entirely too big on her pale face as she looks from me to Nic. I know she's checking for any sign that I'm kidding, but she won't find any. She wants to make a brave stand. I can almost see her internal struggle. A moment later, she gets to her feet and walks to her bedroom. I expect to hear the door slam, but when it shuts softly, it makes me nervous. "I'd rather she kicked the damn thing in," Nic says, echoing my own thoughts as he glances in the direction she disappeared to. "I fully expected some bitching. That was rather disappointing."

I release the breath I wasn't aware I was holding. "She's not in the car yet. That went entirely too easily. She'll probably put a bullet in my head at some point tonight. You get the hugs, and I get the insults." I flip him off when he merely smiles at my jealous sulking.

We're still heckling each other when she returns holding a small suitcase. She's changed into jeans and a dark sweater, along with a pair of combat boots. *Better to kick my ass with.* She seems irritated that I'm still where she left me, but I'm not sure what she was expecting. Maybe me pacing the floor and counting the moments until her return. "For all your talk of urgency, you aren't doing anything to expedite our departure."

Nic yawns loudly and makes a show of stretching before moving into a sitting position. "We should probably think about hitting the road. It'll take us half an hour to reach the compound."

"You call your home 'the compound?'" Nina smirks. "Is this one of those things where a guy with a small pecker gives everything in his life a manly name to compensate for it?"

Nic's laughter turns into a cough as I glare at him before shaking my head at the slip of a girl who defies and insults me at every turn. It had been much more amusing when it was Tony catching this kind of hell from Jacey. I need to get out of here before I do something crazy like drop my pants to prove to Nina that I have no shortcomings in that area whatsoever. "The Moretti compound is Tony's family home," Nic informs her, as he gives me a slight shake of the head over her shoulder. I'm pretty sure that's code for *don't drop your pants, dude.* "We've used it before during a period of unrest. It's very secure and off the grid."

Nina winces. "I don't think he likes me. Maybe you should tell him ahead of time that you're bringing me along. Might save time and a very awkward conversation."

I get to my feet and take Nina's bag from her shoulder and slide it onto mine. "Tony is aware you'll be with us. We would never bring anyone into his home without his knowledge or approval. Plus, it was actually his idea. It's the one place you can go to ground for a while and be completely safe. Both the Morettis and Gavinos will know you're there, but no one in either organization would dare to cross the threshold of Draco Moretti's home to harm you. That would only be done as a declaration of war, and the Gavinos are not suicidal or stupid enough for that."

Without speaking, Nic walks to the door, and I motion for Nina to follow him while I bring up the rear. She hands me her keys, and I lock the door behind us as we move silently toward my BMW. I remove my own keys from my pocket and click to open the doors, then press the button for the ignition. And that's when the world erupts around us. A wall of intense heat pushes us from our feet and flings us through the air like rag dolls. I hear someone screaming, and I think it's Nina. I land hard on my back and immediately roll to the side to survey my surroundings before coming up into a crouch. There's so much smoke that I can barely make anything out. A quick check shows the gun in my ankle holster still in place. I take it in my hand and begin looking for Nic and Nina. I've made it a few feet when I see both Nina's bag on the ground and my cousin shaking his head as he stumbles to his feet. "Can't fucking believe you had a bomb in your car. Whoever did that has some big balls, and I'm going to enjoy cutting them off with the dullest blade I can find."

"Where's Nina?" I whisper urgently. "I thought I heard her cry out right after it happened." As if by silent agreement, we line up back to back with our guns drawn and begin scouting the area. We haven't gone far when I hear coughing. We both freeze, then profanity fills the air in a voice I'd know anywhere. We move in that direction and find her leaning against a tree. Her face is covered in soot, and her clothes haven't fared much better.

Sounding weirdly calm, she asks, "Did your car really just blow up? You didn't do that to scare me, right?"

I give her a look of disbelief that clearly says she's insane. "Belle, I'd never resort to blowing up my fucking X6 to convince you that you're in danger. I'd spank your ass and throw you over my shoulder before I'd destroy my favorite ride."

"We need to get the fuck out of here," Nic hisses under his breath. "I hear sirens, and a crowd is gathering."

"You're not supposed to leave the scene of a crime," Nina points out. "The police will have a lot of questions about this."

"That's why we need to go now," I say grimly as I gently help her up. I put an arm around her shoulders, and the three of us make our way as unobtrusively as possible to Nic's Escalade. I'm on autopilot as Nic and I make a quick sweep of the SUV before opening the doors. Whoever planted the bomb knew what they were doing. The explosion had been controlled. There's no significant damage to any other cars or structures in the area. Although, what looks to be the hood of the X6 is now crushing the hell out of some nearby shrubs. *What the fuck?* Who knew I was here? And how long had they known? *Were they after me, or had they worked out I was watching Nina?* Too many fucking unanswered questions.

She continues to argue as I bundle her into the back seat of Nic's SUV. "It isn't as if they can't trace that burning wreck back to you, Einstein. It might take time, but it can be done. Haven't you watched any of those police shows?"

Between the near-death experience and her nonstop bitching, my skull feels like it's splitting in two. I strive for patience, knowing she's likely even more traumatized now. This hasn't been an easy night for her, and I need to remember that. I turn in my seat, just able to see her outline in the darkness. "Belle, I'm aware they'll run the identification of my car. But right now, we need to get to safety. Whoever planted that bomb may well be lurking around, and I can't risk them using the cover of the crowd to take a shot at one of us. The police will understand when this is explained."

We're both silent for a few moments while Nic calls Sean to give him a rundown of what's happened. Sean Moretti is my father's highest-ranking lieutenant as well as a liaison to the local authorities when needed. That will definitely be necessary now. Asheville, North Carolina, might have its share of crime, but a car explosion on an upscale residential street is pretty rare. There will be questions and plenty of them. When Nic is finished, he chuckles ruefully. "I've gotta say, even Sean was a bit surprised by that news. Normally, nothing throws him off. But his first response was, 'Come again?' I can only imagine what Rutger's reaction will be."

I grimace, knowing my father's temper well. "I'd say it'll involve the word *fuck* a lot. If he's smart, he'll get it out of his system before he goes home, though."

"Hell yeah." Nic shudders. "For such a little thing, your mom is one scary woman."

"She is," I agree. I don't add that she's also the most loving, supportive person I know. She doesn't take any shit from anyone. No doubt it's a major reason my parents have been happily married for so long. They love just as hard as they fight. I've heard that men grow up to marry women like their mothers, and while I've always found that to be a little disturbing, there's no denying she and Nina are a lot alike. *Keep thinking that shit, and you'll never get it up around Nina again.*

I'm more than happy to push that from my mind as Nic slows to make a turn. He rolls the window down and exchanges a few words with the guard at the gate. Then we wait while the vehicle is inspected. Even though we're known here, safety protocol must be followed. The men here are trained by a retired Navy SEAL, and many of them are retired military as well. "Lester is waiting for you at the house," the guard informs us before tipping a hand to his forehead and pushing a button to open the gate.

"This is like something out of a movie," Nina marvels as we pass several armed guards on the three-mile trip to Tony's home.

"Security is tight right now because of the unrest within the Gavino family. Also, Tony knew I'd be coming here, so I assume he added more men to the already sizable crew. The compound is over ten acres of land, so patrolling it is no small task."

Nina takes her safety belt off and moves until she's between our seats. "Don't Tony and Jacey live in an apartment in his club? Or has that changed?"

"What the fuck, Belle? You just tossed out personal information about one of the most powerful men connected to the mafia as if it were nothing. You *cannot* do that."

"He's right, Nina," Nic says, surprising me. He's unusually serious. "Even before this latest development, that would have caused a few raised eyebrows if it got back to the wrong people. But now, what you view as an innocent comment could get you killed. With Franklin gone, you're simply an unknown entity with no one within the Gavinos to stand up for you. At this point, they'd rather eliminate you than have to worry about you."

It irks me a bit when she says softly, "Oh... I see." Have I not said something similar several times already? Yet I can tell she's shaken by Nic's warning. "I hadn't thought of it like that." *What the fuck?* I'd practically drawn her a picture. Is she really that intent on disagreeing with everything I say? *In a word, yes.* I attempt to control my irritation as we come to a stop in front of the house. "But don't a lot of people know about Tony's apartment in the club? Surely, he's... entertained there before."

Nic chuckles wryly, while I resist the urge to beat my head on the dashboard. Can she never simply just toss out the white flag and give in? I'd be so shocked if she did, I'd probably check her for a pulse. "They're not under scrutiny from the wrong people, sweetheart. You are." I see Lester approaching, so I open the door and step out before she can think of a comeback. The older man and I shake hands, then he claps me on the back and then does the same to Nic. His gaze shifts beyond me to where Nina stands a few feet away. "Lester, I'd like you to meet Nina. She's a friend of ours, and I believe Tony told you we'd be staying here for a few days." Even though Lester has Tony's complete trust, I still keep the introductions deliberately vague. I also have no intention of telling him about the car bomb. If Tony decides to bring him into the loop, then I'll trust his judgment, but I don't volunteer information that'll lead to more questions. The past has taught us a hard and deadly lesson about the men who protect us. One traitor is more than capable of bringing an entire organization to its knees. Neither the Morettis nor the Gavinos are immune to such betrayal. Anger surges through me at the thought of Tony's uncle Marcel, but I push the grim memories away. *Now isn't the time for it. Focus.*

"Pleasure, young lady," Lester says briefly as he tips his head respectfully in Nina's direction. Tony has trained him well, so he doesn't ask, nor expect, an explanation for our bedraggled appearances. In the light of the courtyard, I can't help but notice that Nina looks as if she's been dragged through a field full of thorns by her hair. She even has a leaf dangling from one strand. A glance in Nic's direction confirms he hasn't fared much better. Now that the adrenaline is wearing off, I'm aware of several new aches and pains in my body. "Door's open. Let me know if you need anything. Security is tight and the compound is well-covered, so I wouldn't expect any unwanted guests."

"Thanks, Lester." I nod, then turn to put my hand on Nina's back. "Let's get inside. I don't know about you, but I could use a shower and a drink."

"Oh baby, talk dirty to me." She grins before wincing. "Toss in some Advil, and that'll be the best offer I've had in ages."

Nic makes a gagging sound as he motions impatiently at the front door. "If you two can get your hormones under control until later, I'd really appreciate it."

A smart retort is on the tip of my tongue before I remember that he's covering my back. He can't go inside until I do. Were Tony here, we'd both be covering his. It's simply the way of our family. The highest-ranking member must be covered. It's a custom I've never been fond of when it means using someone as a human shield to protect me. But arguing is pointless and will only keep us exposed longer.

The enormity of what's transpired tonight weighs heavily on my mind as the three of us walk wearily into Tony's house. An odd feeling of finality makes me uneasy as Nic closes the door behind us. Did he slam the damn thing, or am I simply imagining how loudly it echoed throughout the empty foyer? Taking Nina into my protection had merely been a precaution before, but now that someone blew my fucking car up, the game has changed significantly. The Morettis will be forced to retaliate. Even if I were some lowly member of the family, an attack would not be tolerated. But considering my rank, this was some serious shit. Sure, it could be argued that Nina was the target, and there is probably some truth to that, but the bomb hadn't been in her car. I was either meant to be the victim or collateral damage. It doesn't really matter. Dead is dead. As I glance at Nina, I'm filled with both rage and guilt. I set these wheels into motion, and there is nothing to do but survive as it plays out. I make a silent vow to both her and myself. I'll do whatever it takes to see that she doesn't pay for the sins of Franklin or his idiot son.

Nor will she pay for mine.

From this point forward, I'll be her human shield, and God help anyone who tries to go through me to get to her.

2

Nina

I'd never want to admit it to him, but if some mafia nutjob is trying to kill me, there's no one I trust more than the brooding man who hasn't said more than three words in the past ten minutes. Marco is like a caged animal as he paces the length of Tony's study. Since arriving about an hour ago, we've all showered and changed out of our dirty clothes. Marco insisted on standing outside the bathroom door while I cleaned up. Then he handed me off to Nic while he did the same. It seems as if my privacy is a thing of the past for a while. In truth, I'm not sure I would want to be alone even if given the choice. I am seriously spooked. Sure, I spent several years in the home of the Gavino family, and I'm not ignorant to the mafia world by any stretch of the imagination, yet I have never thought my life might be in danger. "Dude, could you please stop? You're giving me motion sickness," Nic grumbles as he sets his bottle of water aside to focus on his cousin.

Marco appears surprised as if he forgot we were even in the room with him. At any other time, I'd probably have some dirty thoughts about his ability to focus so single-mindedly, but the whole bomb thing has put a dent in my libido. *But his ass is so amazing in those jeans.* Okay, apparently, I can have a near-death experience and still objectify Marco Moretti a short while later. If he were to ever discover how often he starred in my solo sessions, I'd be forced to move to another country, change my name, and start over again. I've barely been able to keep him at arm's length with my insults. If he has a clue that I want him as much as he claims to desire me, it will be game over. He would use that to get exactly what he wanted, and then I'd be one more woman in a long line who have fallen victim to the charms of the Italian stud, Marco Moretti. And dammit, I don't want to be another groupie. He might not be a rock star, but something is sexy about the air of danger that surrounds him. I'm completely lost in my head when I feel a thump on my shoulder. "Wh—what?" I ask in confusion. Both Marco and Nic are staring at me expectantly. Then I see movement in the doorway. Two Marcos? *A head injury. There can be no other explanation.*

"Are you sure you just gave her Advil?" Nic asks his cousin in amusement. "She looks stoned. I swear if you're hoarding the good stuff, I'm going to be pissed."

I blink a few times, but the other Marco is still there. When he moves from the shadows into the room, I see subtle differences. A big one being the gray at his temples. The pieces fall into place seconds before he reaches Marco's side and pulls him into a hug. "Son, had to come see for myself that you're okay." It's rather amusing to see Nic wearing a respectful expression as he extends a hand to the older man. "Nicoli, thanks for getting word to us so quickly." The three men speak in low tones for a moment and then turn to face me.

Marco gives me a reassuring half-smile before saying, "Nina, this is my father, Rutger Moretti." I'm not sure if I should remain seated, stand, or bow. He is quite possibly one of the most powerful men in the South—if not the world. Anthony Moretti might be famous in Asheville, but little is known about the current head of the Moretti family. Franklin had never attempted to keep a low profile, and that may have made killing him easier to accomplish. I doubt Rutger is so careless.

He surprises me by crossing the room and taking the chair closest to where I'm sitting. "Nina, it's a pleasure. Franklin spoke highly of you." He looks at his son, almost indulgently as he says, "And Marco is a fan as well. I am sorry our first meeting is under such circumstances, though. Franklin was a valued colleague as well as a friend. Many, including myself, will grieve his passing." I notice he makes no mention of Frankie Jr., which isn't surprising. And truthfully, if he had, I would have known his speech was polite bullshit. There is no way any sane person could mourn *his* death. He had been an asshole, but even worse, he'd been a dangerous one. No part of me will miss Frankie Jr., but Franklin—that's more complicated.

"Thank you," I murmur, weirdly tongue-tied around this charismatic man. No wonder Marco's mother is rumored to be so tough. The poor thing probably had to beat the women off her husband with a stick. Even I admit something about him makes you want to sit up a little straighter, smooth your hair down, and let out a breathy giggle. I mentally roll my eyes at my inner dialogue. I really must limit my lusting to one Moretti. The whole father-son thing could get a tad confusing, and it's plain wrong. Naturally, I make a mental note to explore it for my next book idea. While it might not appeal to me, there are undoubtedly many mommy porn lovers out there who'd get off on it. *Those who have no excitement in their own lives and create romantic worlds through their writing. Oh, and who own several vibrators when the inspiration proves to be too stimulating. Can I get an amen?* I nearly laugh aloud at that thought but manage to rein it in. Rutger would probably find my humor ill-timed and offensive. Then Nic might be ordered to stab me and dispose of the body. *Shit! Stop before you make a fool of yourself. Oh crap, he's staring at me. What did he say?*

Nic has his head cocked to the side as he smirks. It's then I realize something horrifying. Oh my God, I'm gripping Rutger's arm so tightly that I'm probably cutting his circulation off. I think I detect a hint of curiosity in his otherwise blank expression. *Think fast!* "I... er, sorry about that. I was so overcome with... grief. Pardon the inappropriate touching. I mean, not in the way that sounded, obviously. There was nothing sexual about it. Just that I shouldn't have touched you at all without invitation since you're the big dog." *Oh, dear God. Shut your mouth, Nina.* Yet I continue driving the train, straight off the cliff, down an embankment, and into a wall. "Well, not a dog as in the woof-woof barking type. More of an alpha, although those are mostly animals too. A bull might be a better representation or even a—"

"Nina," Marco says, sounding pained. "I think he gets it." I feel certain that my face is glowing bright pink right about now. How long would I have gone on if he hadn't stopped me? I cringe thinking about it.

"You're no fun at all," Nic complains. "She was just getting started." He shakes his head as he looks at his boss in disappointment. "She can go for an hour if you let her. It's hysterical."

Before Rutger can respond, there's a knock on the door, and as one, the men are instantly alert. It's an impressive sight to see. *If they'd pulled their guns, my nipples would have hardened. Now that could be a great line in my book too.* "It's Lester," a voice calls out. "We've got a little situation at the main gate. It's nothing I can't handle, but I want to see if a visitor is expected first."

"You can come in, Lester," Marco instructs.

When the older man steps inside, he nods respectfully. "There's a Ms. Gavino raising hell, demanding to see Ms. Nina."

"Minka?" I ask in surprise. I get to my feet, wondering what could have possibly brought my friend here. How did she even know where to find me? *This is Minka. There's nothing she can't do, remember?* There's dead silence for a long moment, then Lester inclines his head once in affirmation of my question.

"This could be a trap," Marco warns. "Let's check the video and see." He walks over to the desk and pushes a button. A nearby wall panel slides to the side, revealing a bank of monitors. Another click and there's a sound from the one that I assume is at the front gate.

And there she is, my blonde best friend, looking very much like an avenging angel in what appears to be all black. "Listen here, you fucking rent-a-Joe. If I don't see Nina Gavino in five minutes flat, I'm gonna plant the heel of my boot up your fat ass." Putting her hands on her hips, she adds, "If you don't believe me, then you wait and see. I warn you, though, you'll be shitting manmade materials for a damn month."

"Yep, that would be her all right," Nic mutters distastefully. I don't know why, but those two loathe each other. Considering they're from different families, I have no idea when they've even spent that much time together. I'd asked Minka, but she had been unusually close-mouthed about Nic. I even joked about him ignoring her Facebook request or something silly along those lines, and she glared at me for so long that I dropped the subject and never broached it again. I love Minka like a sister, but I'm smart enough to understand that pissing her off is a bad idea. I've seen her plant a knee in more than one man's balls, so I have no desire to test her patience. I don't need a broken vagina. After all, one day I might use it again. *A girl can always dream.*

"Have her escorted in," Rutger orders, taking me by surprise. I expected she'd be turned away, regardless of her threats. And I'm not so certain that I want more mayhem to deal with right now. "I believe we should hear Ms. Gavino out since she's gone to great trouble to find Nina."

"I think a muzzle and a leash are a better plan," Nic grumbles.

"Nicoli," Rutger chides. "You're speaking of Nina's friend. And from what I just witnessed, it would be prudent not to piss her off."

"I've got twenty on her making you cry like a baby." Marco smirks. "Personally, I'd be curious to see how she gets those heels in *your* ass." Frowning, he quickly adds, "On second thought, that might be a little too much for me." I bite back a grin at his words. His sense of humor is so flipping sexy. *Roll your tongue back in.*

A nearby door slams loudly, and we all jump yet again. Then Lester is back, escorting my frowning best friend. I notice the way the men take in her leather-clad figure, and for the first time, I feel a twinge of envy. I'm short and curvy, with far too much ass. And she's tall and voluptuous. *Get over yourself and stop being such a damn girl.* I swear she snarls when she spots Nic, and the room sizzles with tension. Then she sees me and hurls herself in my direction. I barely have time to squeak in surprise before I'm locked in her arms with my face pressed between her tits. "Oh my God, I've been so fucking worried about you. Ever since this shit went down, it's beyond weird at the home base. I told Daddy if anything happened to you, I'd blow the place up myself. Then I heard on the police scanner that there was an explosion on *your* street. I nearly had a heart attack, Ni." She has always called me a shortened version of my name, and I, in turn, do the same with her.

"Gee, what stopped you?" Nic mutters under his breath, but we all hear him. Minka whips around, and I'm half afraid she'll rip his dick off, but she takes the high road and settles for a withering glare. I think we're all secretly disappointed, but he's probably not out of the woods yet. She has a long memory.

She appears to notice Rutger for the first time, and she whistles through her teeth. "Wow, the Moretti big guy is here. Shit, this must be worse than I thought. No offense and all, dude, but I heard you even have someone take a dump for you so you don't have to leave your office."

Marco sounds as if he's choking, and Nic isn't much better. The man whose bathroom habits are in question is laughing. Literally shaking with mirth. And boy, does it move his sexy factor up several notches. I'm not the only one who thinks so because Minka lifts her brows and wiggles them at me, letting me know she approves. "I'm sorry to disappoint you, Ms. Gavino"—Rutger grins, flashing pearly white teeth—"but I handle all... personal matters myself."

"That's a relief." She nods. "Call me Minka. I'd rather limit the number of times per day I'm forced to hear my surname. Not to mention, right now it's better to be a Smith than a Gavino." She leans back and crosses her arms over her chest. "So what in the hell is going on? I can't imagine that Nina took a drive through the country and, on a whim, decided to drop in to the Moretti compound. Which leads me to believe that you guys brought her here. I'll even toss you the benefit of the doubt and say you're attempting to protect her. If that's the case, why would you let a Gavino—of all gangster people—in without so much as frisking me? That's just bad police work. Have you never watched *Godfather* or *The Sopranos*? Even the nanny or gardener could bust a cap in your ass before you know what's happening."

Nic appears bored rather than pissed when he says, "You went through three different scans on your way to the house, along with one at the front door. We know everything—even what kind of panties you're wearing." When she appears skeptical, he adds, "By the way, isn't leather uncomfortable when you're going commando?"

Her lips twist, and then she shrugs. "I'll let that pass since I'm rather impressed. I've heard Tony is a real technology freak." She takes a seat on the leather sofa and tugs on my arm until I do the same. "Now, what are we going to do about this mess? My daddy is likely to kill me when he discovers I knocked my guard out, so my time is limited. Normally, I'd blame it on you guys, but with all that's going on right now, I wouldn't do that to my worst enemy."

"That's very much appreciated, Minka." Rutger motions to Marco and Nic, and they all take nearby chairs. "Unfortunately, due to the uncertainty of what's transpired recently, the sharing of information would be unwise." He raises his hand when she bristles in indignation. "Surely, you understand. You're not new to our way of life. Even with the best of alliances, this type of thing would be frowned upon. But considering what's happened, it's impossible. I believe that you're only looking out for Nina's welfare, and I commend you for it. I give you my word that we will do the same. She is with us for that very reason."

"I don't like this at all," Minka huffs out in frustration.

I place my hand over hers and give it a reassuring squeeze. "I'll be okay. You need to get back home before you really get into trouble. It's not safe for you to be out alone right now, and you know it. You shouldn't have come, Min, but I love you for it."

"Nicoli will see you home." His phone rings as he utters the last word, and he removes it from his suit pocket. He frowns as he glances at the caller ID before clicking a button. "Ray, what can I do for you?" Minka stiffens as she hears her father's name. Of course, it could be someone else, but the way Rutger is staring at my friend, I assume her suspicions are correct. "Yes, she's here of her own accord. I have a man bringing her back. Fuck." His abrupt change of dialogue has us all moving closer to the edge of our seats. Tension pours off him in waves as he listens for a moment before saying tensely, "I understand. Keep me updated."

"That was my dad," Minka states calmly, but I don't miss the slight tremor in her voice. She's not afraid of much, but she loves her family and friends fiercely. Given recent events, even she isn't immune to nerves.

"It was." Rutger inclines his head slightly. "Your uncle Don is dead, along with your bodyguard, who I believe was also your cousin Seth."

"Fuck me," Marco hisses, looking as stunned as the rest of us. "What in the hell is going on? Multiple hits on the Gavinos and an attempt on a Moretti? Where is this coming from?" His genuine bewilderment gives me cold chills. I prefer his usual arrogance to this uncertainty. If he's unsettled, then shit just got real.

"They think it was me, don't they?" Minka mutters in a neutral tone. "No need to sugarcoat it. There's too much paranoia right now not to jump to conclusions, even if they are asinine."

I get to my feet and do a little dance. "Woot, woot. Looks like I'm off the hook thanks to you. Way to take one for the team, buddy." Minka merely rolls her eyes at my display, but the guys obviously think I'm insane. "Too soon?"

I ask the room in general, but Minka holds up her fingers, showing a small space between them. "Maybe a tad. After all, I am short another two family members." And even though it bordered on insensitive, I accomplished my goal of breaking the tension in the room. Speaking ill of the dead isn't usually advisable, but Minka's twisted sense of humor appreciates what most don't.

"You hated them," I point out. "You called Don a human butt plug and Seth a fart sniffer or was it an ass licker? No, there was definitely some sniffing involved. Armpit? Nipple? Crotch? Crap, am I close?"

"Belle," Marco interrupts, sounding pained.

"Please stop her before she goes on another tangent. I'd rather stand blindfolded on the Gavino front lawn than go through that again," Nic groans. Although, I know he actually likes it when I ramble. Marco hasn't been alone every time he's dropped by my place unannounced. Often, Nic has been there as well. During those times, they both came in and made themselves at home. Nic divided his time between making fun of Marco for being love-sick, picking on me for anything he could come up with, and, of course, lying on my damned sofa as if he owned the place. Secretly, I've been thankful for the other man's presence because it's taken the pressure off. I've refused to give in to my attraction to Marco, and if we were alone for too long together, I didn't trust that I'd be able to maintain indifference. He's just too... impressive.

Flipping a hand in Marco's direction, Minka asks, "What's with the whole Belle thing?"

In a synchronized move that has both Minka and me gawking, Marco, Nic, and Rutger, say, "*Beauty and the Beast.*"

"You're shitting me, right?" Minka laughs. "Bunch of hard-asses like yourselves watch Disney movies?" Marco and Nic both appear to be staring in fascination at some random spot on the wall, while I do my best not to grab my phone and google the person who I apparently remind Marco of. I vaguely remember seeing the movie as a child, but that was years ago. "You know, slick," Minka adds, obviously still addressing Marco, "if Nina is the beauty in the scenario, then you're the beast."

Marco's eyes lock on to mine, never looking away as he answers softly, "Was that ever in doubt?" *Oh, God. I think I was just Mr. Darcy'ed. That smolder.*

Rutger clears his throat, effectively drawing his son's focus from me. "The banter is rather entertaining; however, we need to get back to business. Even though there is an argument to be made for safety in numbers, I fear that's too predictable. Until we have a better understanding of the scope of the situation, I think we should split up. I realize none of us are in the position to go underground for any lengthy amount of time. We have a company to run and jobs to do. Son, you will watch over Nina as planned, and Nicoli, you will be entrusted with Minka's safety." I wince, waiting for the objections to begin, yet Minka and Nic are strangely silent. *Great, while war rages all around them, these two will be fucking like bunnies.* In her defense, though, if I said the word, Marco would happily do me. He has never tried to hide the fact that he wants me. But considering his reputation, that doesn't give me a lot of bragging rights. After all, many, many, many women have been there. If Don was the human butt plug, then Marco is the human dick. I bite my lip to keep from giggling at the images that pop into my head. "All right, if there is nothing more to add, then I'm going to the office. With only a few hours left until daylight, Nic and Minka will remain here with you, Marco. We can discuss any problems later." Rutger says a brief goodbye and leaves as silently as he arrived.

"His father is fucking hot." Minka sighs, elbowing me. "Don't pretend you didn't notice. If I had to choose him or Marco, I'd need to draw straws. That would be like trying to pick between a thong or bikini. Both would feel good against your ass. Know what I mean?" *Um, actually, no, I don't. There's been no ass action for me, sister. No front action recently either. Dammit.*

Marco drops his head. "That's one of the most disturbing things I've ever heard about my father, and that's saying something. In the future, can you refrain from mentioning us and anal in the same conversation?"

"Who knew gangsters were so uptight." I sigh. "Especially one who has unzipped for half the female population in the state."

As Minka and I toss zingers out, I barely notice when Marco and Nic step out of the room, but Minka does. She stops midsentence with a disbelieving shrug. "Can you believe this shit? We're under house arrest, and our jailors are hot enough to make a nun's panties wet. I swear, I don't know how I'm going to make it without letting Nic bang me. And there is no way you'll hold out against Marco. It was different when you could hide in your apartment and pretend you weren't home. But now, you'll be with him twenty-four seven. I predict that before the week is over, he will be the third man you've slept with. Hell, you need to do it just to increase that number to an average range. Don't you want to experience mind-blowing sex before you're too old to enjoy it? And that's one thing I can guarantee with Marco. He will rock your world." I don't bother to remind her that I didn't always hide. Although I learned after the first few times not to mention to her when Nic was along on one of Marco's visits. *Why does she pretend to hate him?*

"That's what I'm afraid of," I admit. "And it has very little to do with sex."

Suddenly serious, Minka says, "You can't romanticize Marco Moretti, Ni. He's not a character in your book. Sure, it's possible for a bad boy to fall in love and reform his ways, but Marco goes beyond the typical guy sowing his wild oats all over town. He has mob lizards throwing themselves at him from every direction. It would take a formidable person to resist that kind of lure. Those bimbos can probably put both legs behind their head while performing multiple blowjobs, and you can damn well bet they take it in the ass. How can a normal woman compete with that?"

"Maybe I can do all of that as well," I snap, but we both know I'm lying. I can't bring myself to write anal scenes, much less wave the green ass-flag and tell Marco to go for it. I realize that Minka is trying to save me from getting my heart broken, but her graphic description has hit me harder than I care to admit. Have I been harboring some type of secret crush on Marco? *Who hasn't? Everything about him screams carnal and erotic. Everything. His eyes. His smile. His arrogance.* But the crush stops now. Minka is right; there is no world where he will ever be my Prince Charming. I am the girl who writes about the things I've always longed to find, but unless heartache is one of my future goals, I need to keep my guard up and my panties in place. Whether I want to admit it, he's dangerous to my health, and it has nothing to do with his job and everything to do with my reaction to him. *He's gotten to me. Dammit, how did I let this happen?* There's no disputing the fact that he's hot. *That's the understatement of the century.* But even more than that, he's smart, funny, and so damned loyal to his family. Even though there's nothing about his way of life that I approve of, the way they all have each other's backs is admirable. *He has mine as well, and I'm nothing to him. I am neither Moretti nor Gavino. I'm an outsider.* I've joked about honor among thieves, but in his case, there is truth there. I sense the strict code within him. Maybe it's my hormones talking, but I sense so much more to him than what he shows the world. *Says every woman who has ever thought she could change a man. He's mafia. I can't be my mother. I cannot fall for a man who is married to the family.* As I attempt to hide my panic from Minka, one thought keeps swirling in my head: *God help me if he ever finds out I have feelings for him.*

3

Marco

It could be argued that the occupants of this room have more power combined than the president of the United States. I'm not positive of that, but it should certainly make the right people nervous that current and past Moretti power players are sitting in a soundproof conference room. Tony is at one end of the table, while my father is at the other. Former wonder boy and the man who helped Draco build this empire, Lee Jacks, is on the right, and Nic and I are to the left. It's a rare situation that brings us together at the office, as both Tony and Lee are no longer active within the family. The fact that they've managed to distance themselves from the daily operations is a testament to the power they wield because the old stereotypes of there being only one way out of the mafia are basically true, even in this modern age. It's not like your normal job where you quit if you're unhappy. Nor is there a gold watch and a shitty retirement check when you pack your desk after years of slaving away at some thankless job. The most you can really hope for is to move up within the organization where you're in the position to call the shots—somewhat. There is always oversight, though. I am at the top, but I still answer to my father and always will.

And we both answer to my mother. Now there is a woman with some clout. "You carried out the hit personally on Franklin and his son?" Lee asks, pulling my thoughts from where they'd strayed momentarily. Lee wasn't personally consulted or informed, but I'm not surprised at his assumption. He's been around long enough to make some damn accurate guesses.

Before I can respond, my father says, "I ordered the terminations. I take no pleasure in Franklin's death, but it was unavoidable."

"Agreed." Tony sighs. "Franklin was informed on three different occasions that his son was involved with human traffickers."

I lean forward in my chair and slide a folder in front of Lee. "We'd been tracking his movements for months. There is no doubt in my mind that he planned to use our warehouses and resources to get his side business off the ground. None of us can afford the type of scrutiny that something like that could bring down on our heads. The day before their deaths, the talk on the street had gone from chatter to fucking screams. True to form, Frankie was too damned stupid and lazy to cover his tracks while he was organizing, much less when he was operational. It had disaster written all over it in red and fucking underlined."

"If there were an alternative, we would have used it. But Franklin's misguided loyalty to his son ultimately necessitated their demise." The death of one of my father's closest allies has been hard on him. I see a weariness that wasn't there a month ago, and I hear it in his voice as he finishes speaking. As much as we've tried to move the family away from shit like this, there will always be something that forces our hand, and none of us in this room like it. More often than not, it hasn't been necessary to raise a hand against an enemy. Even with the Morettis, there is a higher power—and I'm not talking God here. If we don't act or delegate it out, then we will be perceived as weak, which would have far-encompassing ramifications. It's in everyone's best interest for the Morettis to remain firmly in control. We keep those who would attempt to overrun the city in check. No moves are made here by outsiders without our consent. The alliance with the Gavinos is a rarity in our world. Sure, it's not unusual for different families to come together briefly if there is a deal lucrative enough for both parties. But this lasts no longer than is strictly necessary. Tony's father, Draco, had done that very thing with the Gavinos on more than one occasion. But my father had cemented a working relationship with them, mainly because he went to school with Raymond Gavino, and they'd remained on friendly terms. Franklin and Raymond had been intrigued by our successful transition into mostly legitimate avenues.

Lee leans back in his chair as he processes what he's just heard. Finally, he nods once in understanding. None of us at this table are new to this game, or naïve to how things must be, and certainly not Lee. He was the protégé of both Draco and his best friend, Victor Falco. This man has seen or heard it all, so very little would shock him anymore. "Have accusations been made?"

"I don't know about you, but blowing Marco's ride all to hell seems a bit like finger-pointing to me," Nic quips. "Nothing says *I think you're guilty* quite like seeing your hood fly past your head."

His comic relief may not always be timely, but I think we all appreciate it now. That we can even joke about something that could have had a dire outcome is a testament to the shit we've seen through the years. "Yeah, that was a tad more than a slap on the wrist. And I washed the fucking thing this morning. Every damn time I do that, it brings bad karma. Either rain, bird shit, or a bomb."

Tony grins as he tosses a pen at me. "Time to look for a new insurance company. Despite what they say, I'm betting Nationwide will *not* be on your side this time." There's laughter at Tony's use of the well-known insurance slogan.

"Damn, that was a good one." Nic frowns. "I wish I'd thought of it first."

"Boys." My father rolls his eyes as he attempts to bring us back to the business at hand. There's no real irritation in his tone, though. Without the ability to laugh at what would scare the hell out of the average person, we'd have all succumbed to a stress-related heart attack long ago. The tone in this room would be a *vastly* different one had one of us been killed. If that happened, the men joking here tonight would be lethal. *Bloodthirsty.* "I've spoken to our contact at police headquarters and what remains of the car will be brought here. I doubt there is any evidence left due to the heat, but we'll go over it anyway." He turns to Nic, and asks, "I understand you were outside for a good length of time alone. You saw nothing unusual?" It's more of a statement than a question. We all know that the Gavinos aren't likely to be planting a bomb in a car on a public street at any hour of the day. That's shit that only a novice or an idiot would do. *Someone like Frankie Jr.*

Nic shakes his head. "Not a thing. It could have been in there for a while. That shit is so advanced now, it can be programmed on a timer, for a certain number of ignition fires, or when the fucking heat is turned on. So many options. Unless more of the device is left than I think, it'll be damn near impossible to know for certain. If I had to guess, I'd say it had only been there for the past twenty-four hours. Whoever planted it was likely hedging their bets that Marco would go to Nina after Franklin's death. Considering I usually pick him up, the car stays garaged a great deal of the time, but even the best security can be breached, especially when it's unmanned."

My father nods before looking at me. "Put the word out that until further notice, all vehicles are to be checked before they're started."

"This feels too obvious," Tony muses thoughtfully. "Sure, the Gavinos have a few loose cannons, but the only one stupid enough to have done something like this is dead."

"Exactly. But it would have to be a person who's in the know on both ends. We've had an alliance with the Gavinos for a while now."

"Wouldn't take a genius to understand the ramifications of Franklin's death," Lee points out. "But you're correct. Enough paranoia would exist for the Morettis to automatically be their number-one suspect."

"I hate to say this," Tony says, "but this is exactly why a long-term alliance cannot exist between two such powers."

"I, too, believe they've outstayed their welcome here," Lee says. "Not only do we have our families to consider, but the people of this city as well. A full-blown battle between the families would put too many innocents in harm's way. We co-exist with the authorities because we protect our backyard. We cannot allow others to trample on that which we've carefully cultivated."

All eyes turn to my father since he has not only maintained the link with the Gavinos, but is also the man responsible for approving our next steps. He absently pats his jacket pocket and then frowns. "Fuck, I wish I still smoked."

"So do I." Tony grins. "I can't tell you how many times I still reach for a pack only to find it's not there."

I get to my feet and pour us all a generous measure of bourbon from the nearby bar. "It's not the same, but at least it'll take the edge off," I say before tossing mine back.

When my father has finished his, he leans forward, staring at Tony intently. "I agree with what both you and Lee are saying. I've known this day was coming for a while now. Hence Franklin and his son's elimination. There are those within the Gavino family who will resist their eviction from our area, and we must be prepared for what they'll do when they're pushed out. Now, more than ever, you must take precautions to protect your family first, and then your assets. The more seasoned Gavino soldiers wouldn't dare come against a Moretti or anyone connected to us, but there's always some punk eager to fast-track up the ladder. They have no clue they'll be signing their own death warrant."

"They have never been as vulnerable as they are right now," I say as I look at Nic. "Regardless of the hostilities at times, there have been friendships of sorts formed. How will those be handled? Just right off the top of my head, there's Minka, her father, Raymond, and Nina."

"Nina isn't officially tied to the Gavinos," my father states. "So this doesn't apply to her. Unless, of course, she develops some misplaced sense of loyalty to them." He leans forward, his expression grave as he adds, "Ray and Minka are a different matter." I see Nic freeze and open his mouth, but my father continues speaking before he can utter the first word of protest. "I'm not saying there isn't room for compromise where they're concerned. It depends largely on Ray's willingness to bend. His cooperation will go a long way toward preventing additional loss of life."

"He can be reasonable," Lee muses. "Especially when it involves the well-being of his family."

"That's true." Tony nods. "But we must also be prepared for him to be pissed and out for revenge. He's not a stupid man. He'll figure out quickly that his brother's death is likely no coincidence when we begin pushing them out. How do you plan to play this? Set up a meeting with him or put the wheels in motion and see where everyone falls?"

"That's the million-dollar question," I reply. "Issuing a warning ahead of time is a courtesy among friends, but you have to damn well hope they don't use it against you. Do we trust him not to sound the alarm within his organization? Up until this moment, I'd call him an ally if asked. But that doesn't change the fact that he's not one of us."

My father grimaces, and I know what's coming. "No, he's not. But... we have his daughter. He's devoted to her, and she's loyal to Nina. Trust me when I say that it's not a card I want to play and I hope it's not necessary. I've never agreed with dragging families into our wars. There should always be rules that gentlemen follow. Otherwise, chaos will soon reign."

"Sometimes it's unavoidable when there are no other avenues available," Lee says grimly. "The difference is they will not be physically harmed by us."

"No, they will not," my father responds without hesitation. "But Ray cannot be certain of that, and it may be the leverage we need to sway him. I believe he wants a way out of the family, and if possible, I'll help him achieve that. For a price."

"You have no clue who you're dealing with," Nic groans. "There is no way Minka won't tear the place apart when she gets wind of this. We better be ready with a stun gun or a sedative. One strong enough to put a fucking horse down." Then he looks at me and lifts a brow sarcastically. "And if you believe Nina won't be right there beside her, you're deluded, my friend. They might not be blood sisters, but you can bet your ass they'll band together against us."

"I am married, Nicoli," my father murmurs in amusement. "My wife has given me many lessons in how women think, so I have anticipated this. That's why they'll be kept apart until this is settled. We cannot afford to have them going rogue and fucking things up at a crucial time. I had thought to have Marco and Nina stay at the compound, but for now, I'd rather keep Minka there. Nicoli, you'll stay there at night when you're not needed. We'll direct a few of our men to provide reinforcements for those already in place. Tony, I realize this is your home, but I hope you will allow us to use it for a while. Naturally, we'll compensate your staff."

"That's not necessary." Tony shrugs. "We aren't there often, so it's no imposition. If there's a problem Lester can't handle, let me know, and I'll see to it."

As they discuss security with Lee, Nic elbows me in the side. "Why am I getting stuck with the defiant one? I'm man enough to admit that hellcat scares me. How do we know she didn't kill her guard? Kind of ironic that she admits to knocking him out, then bam, he's dead. Can you imagine what a case of PMS will do to her? She will murder us all in our sleep."

"You're such a whiny little bitch." I smirk. "Afraid of a girl. Just guard the family jewels and wear a bulletproof vest. What's the odds she'll land a kill-shot?"

"Laugh it up, cupcake," he says. "But don't say I didn't warn you about Nina. Have you forgotten our first meeting? Because I certainly haven't. She had a gun inches away from my dick, and her hand was as steady as yours."

"If she wanted me dead, she had plenty of opportunities to make it happen, considering I was practically unconscious in her apartment for hours. I like my odds here. You, on the other hand, might be in trouble. I'd advise you to catch naps while you're away from the compound because I don't think I'd let my guard down if Minka is anywhere near."

He gives me a slightly demented look that is equal parts sarcasm and irritation. "Gee, thanks so much for that comforting speech. Any more of your reassurances and I'll be sitting in my car like a pussy instead of going inside." He smacks a hand to his forehead before adding, "Oh wait, that was you. You know, you kind of owe me. If I hadn't been there to kick your ass into gear, whoever blew the bimmer might have simply decided to put you out of your misery."

It registers a split second later than the room is entirely too silent. When I glance around, I see the other men following our conversation with obvious enjoyment. *Fuck my life.* Nic's choked laughter tells me he's been aware of it all along. *The bastard will so pay for that.*

"No shame in being terrified of an angry woman," Tony drawls in amusement. "We've all stood on the other side of the door for longer than necessary to avoid that very thing."

Lee shakes his head in Nic's direction. "It's a truly stupid man who doesn't have second and third thoughts in that situation. There have been times when I'd rather take my chances in an exploding car than face Jade's ire."

"Now we've established Nicoli's lack of intelligence in matters of the opposite sex, let's wrap this up," my father adds dryly. He studies each of us for a long moment, all traces of humor gone. "Protect what's yours," he says. "We will regroup as necessary. Tony and Lee, let's touch base daily for now. You might be officially retired from the daily operations here, but knowledge is power—and protection." Both agree without hesitation, knowing that my father wouldn't make the request unless it was in their best interest. "Nicoli, escort Minka back to the compound. I'd send her with some of our men, but she might cause fewer problems since she knows you." I hear Nic's faint groan but resist the urge to heckle him since I'm bound to be next up on my father's agenda. "And son, take Nina to your place. I've already placed extra people there for the foreseeable future."

I get to my feet as the meeting ends. Nic mutters something about using the bathroom, but we both know he's putting off the inevitable. "Chicken shit." I smirk as he walks out the door. Hell, I force myself not to take the fucking stall right next to him. Only the image of someone discovering us cowering in fear from two women keeps me from doing just that. My father holds up a hand, motioning for me to remain behind after Tony and Lee leave. I drop back into my chair as he shuts the door and takes the seat that Nic vacated.

"This is going to be like a fucking land mine going forward," he says. "I already feel as if I have one foot in concrete and the other in dog shit."

We laugh even though neither of us finds anything that's happened the least bit amusing. "I'm right there with you," I acknowledge as a wave of pure mental fatigue washes over me. I'm the kind of exhausted that no amount of sleep will cure. The only thing that could possibly ease it would be a resolution without further bloodshed. And that's about as likely as Santa dropping down my chimney on Christmas Eve.

"I know I don't have to keep reminding you of this, son, but we have to exercise the utmost care going forward. If word gets out, it'll be bad for everyone, but where we're concerned, it'll be catastrophic. Not only would our enemies be at our door, but our friends and family as well."

"You're not telling me anything I haven't already thought of a million times," I mutter uneasily. "We may have had few options, but the potential fallout keeps me awake every fucking night. We've betrayed the trust of so many people—fuck, I grew up with a big majority of them. In even the best-case scenario, how could there possibly be a good outcome to this mess?" Turning to face him, I ask bleakly, "Tell me in what world we'll ever feel good about what we've done and continue to do?"

If I expect him to roll out one of his inspirational pep talks, I'm sadly mistaken. Hell, I'd want to punch him if he did. We both know you can't take a frog and turn it into a prince—no fucking way. "We won't," he says flatly. "In every game, there must be a loser, no matter how much you wish differently. There will be regrets and doubts. As much as we hate it, there is no turning back now. We passed that point long ago. There is only one direction for us—forward."

I pick up a pen from in front of me and toss it across the table in frustration. "The worst part of this whole fucked-up mess is deceiving Tony, Lee, and Nic. They've had our backs through thick and thin, and we're planting a knife in theirs as a fucking thank you." We're both silent for a moment, each lost in our thoughts. The air around us is full of tension, but it's not directed at each other. We went into this with our eyes wide open. I doubt either of us was aware of how bad it would feel to fuck over the people we cared about—but my father is right, there is no turning back now.

"This is about the worst possible time to be on babysitting duty," he says wryly. "I don't know Nina well, but I observed enough of the interaction between her and Minka to realize they could be trouble." I don't bother to defend her as he's merely stating the obvious.

"Undoubtedly." I nod in agreement. "When they're together, Minka's personality diverts attention from Nina's. But make no mistake, Nina is a hellion when she wants to be. She has her sweet moments, but they're usually only when you're knocking on death's door... after being poisoned."

"And that is precisely why I've extended our protection to her. She could have handled things very differently when she found you that day, but she put herself at risk to help you. I always repay a marker when it's called in—especially if I create the storm they need to be sheltered from. I don't worry that much about Nic with Minka. She may damn well attempt to chop his dick off and feed it to him, but he isn't privy to or involved in what you and I are. You can't tell what you don't know."

"I'll watch myself," I say easily, but I'm smart enough to know it won't be that simple. If Nina were to find out everything I've done, she wouldn't stop at blowing my dick off. She'd probably kill me and revive me, only to repeat the process all over again. She may look like an angel, but there are horns on that halo.

My father chuckles as he shoots me a pitying glance. "I said something similar to a friend of mine when I met your mother. There have been many times through the years that I wish I'd run in the other direction. I love that woman, but she'd have the pope drinking and cursing in less than a week. If nothing else, she certainly taught me to never take anyone at face value. Everyone is made up of many layers, and you never truly know who they are until you've peeled most of them away." He grins wryly before adding, "When that happens, it may well scare the hell out of you."

"Hey, that's my sweet little mother you're talking about," I say, attempting to keep a straight face.

"Hell, I love that she can bake cookies while describing in vivid detail how she'd kill you if you fuck up. That right there is a rare quality. She's had my balls sweating on more than one occasion, and I'm man enough to admit it."

"I'd call you a pussy, but you'd probably kick my ass," I joke. "And she's had the same effect on me too many times to count." He gets that soft grin that only ever appears when he's thinking of my mother. I might give him a hard time about it, but if I ever marry, I hope to find what they have. Some might consider their relationship volatile, but I recognize it for what it is: passionate. There is the typical kind of devotion, and then there is the type that a fortunate few have. No-holds-barred, crazy, hard love. *I want that.* Wait—what? Before I can finish processing that insane thought, I'm discounting it as absurd. Becoming seriously involved with a woman would have been dangerous before, but now, it's likely a death sentence for both of us. The distraction could get me killed, and the unlucky object of my affection would have a target on her back within hours.

Then why is Nina here?

What else could I do?

My motives are mostly innocent where she's concerned, but with bringing her under my wing, am I putting her in even more danger? *You started this whole fucked-up mess. You put her at risk for your own selfish purposes.* "I had no choice, dammit." When my father looks at me in confusion, I realize I said that out loud. *Fuck.*

In that eerie way that both he and my mother have, he appears to read my thoughts perfectly. "There are always options, son, even if you don't like them. But there are also consequences to every decision you make. At times, good outcomes simply aren't possible. In those instances, you protect your inner circle as best you can and recognize that there will be collateral damage."

"You make that sound easy," I say incredulously. "We're not talking about getting a damn stain on your favorite shirt. Our bad day means loss of lives—potentially many of them. Who appointed us as the judge, jury, and executioner? How do we decide who lives or dies in this scenario? Draw straws? Best two out of three?" I snap my fingers in mock excitement before saying, "I've got it. Rock, paper, scissors. Or in our case, bullet, knife, or ax. It's high time we invent our own type of game, right? Hell, imagine the fun with Mafia Monopoly. Beats bingo any day."

I see his eye twitch, another sign of stress. We're on the same team here, so I'm not sure why I'm taking my guilt and frustration out on him. There'd been no gun held to my head. I was in this predicament of my own free will. So why does a part of me blame him for it? *I'll make some lucky shrink very rich one day.* "If you need me to be the bad guy, then I will. It's certainly a role I'm used to playing." His voice is heavy when he adds, "If there were a way to let you out of this, I'd do it. But if you walk now, you'll lose what few options you currently have available. They're not much, I know, but your name may well be the only thing that keeps Nina alive. You'd still be a Moretti. But without the family behind you, that's like a king without a castle. As an outsider, you'd be too busy trying to cover your own ass to take care of anyone else. And if you think it's hard to distinguish between friend and foe now, then imagine what it would be then." *Fuck, I hate that he's right.*

"It's not that difficult to picture," I mutter, "considering we're doing something very similar to most everyone in our life." Then I pause and take a deep breath. This man has always deserved and will always deserve my respect. *He has lived through many losses...* Before he can say more, I sit forward and place a hand on his shoulder. "You're right, of course. I needed to blow off some steam, and you're my only outlet for it. Sucks to be you sometimes, doesn't it?"

"More than you think." He smiles faintly, but the strain is still there. *I'm such an asshole.* "We'll get through this. That's about all I can promise you, other than the unpleasant fact that things will disintegrate rapidly from this point forward. Fuck, they already are. Take Nina, get her settled in at your place, and unwind for a few hours. Tomorrow, we must have our game faces on and be ready for whatever is thrown in our path. And remember, as much as you love Nic—"

"I know," I snap in irritation. "I've been hiding that we fucked him over for ages now. Why are you suddenly concerned I'll let something slip?"

"You didn't fuck Nic over. If anything, you protected him. He'll just never know it. And I worry because there's more to lose now," he says flatly. "Your attention will also be divided." He gets to his feet and takes a few steps before turning to face me once more. "You may care about

this girl, but you better make damn sure she's not the death of us all."
With that final warning, he's gone, and I'm left in a room that is far too
quiet. What I wouldn't give for the freedom to get sloppy drunk with
my only bad decision being a one-night stand with a stage-5 clinger.
Always wear a condom, and don't call a woman the wrong name. Life had
seemed much simpler then.

Why am I still sitting here? *Waiting for a fucking miracle? Divine inter-*
vention? A visit from Santa? I should be thrilled at the prospect of having
Nina all to myself. Isn't this what I've wanted for a year now? If I were
an ordinary man, I'd make the most of it. But I'm not—and I never will
be. Nina thinks I'm little more than a mafia thug, and she has nothing
but disdain for that way of life. Little does she know—it's so much
worse than she could ever imagine. No, if being mafia was my greatest
sin, I'd push that shit aside and turn on the charm. I attempt to swallow
a lump the size of a basketball suddenly wedged in my throat. Because I
know beyond a shadow of a doubt that when this is over, she'll hate me.
I made choices long before she came into the picture, and all I can do is
toss my chips in the air and see where they fall—and hope to God we're
all still alive when the last hand has been played. I cannot and will not
risk those around me who have already made enough sacrifices. *"You*
may care about this girl, but you better make damn sure she's not the death of
us all." As usual, my father is right on the money. But I will not allow his
words to become prophetic. Not on my watch.

Nina

Minka has been unusually quiet since we arrived at the Moretti offices.
Marco and Nic casually escorted us to a comfortable sitting area
complete with overstuffed sofas and a television that covers half of one
wall. It should have been relaxing, if not for it feeling more like a gilded
cage. We hadn't been told not to leave the room, but the guards outside
the door might as well be holding up signs. Under the circumstances,
it's understandable. Not many organizations would give free rein to a
couple of outsiders, and certainly not the mafia. It's nothing short of
impressive—and downright scary—that we were even allowed through

the door. I'm so lost in my thoughts that I nearly jump out of my skin when Minka drops down next to me. I swear, she moves so damn quietly that it's unnerving at times. She leans her head on my shoulder, surprising me with the unusual show of affection. We might hug at times, but we're not really the cuddling type. "Just go with it," she whispers. "Come a little closer so we can't be overheard but try to act normal."

"What are we doing?"

"I have a weird feeling. Something is going on, and I don't fucking like it. And you can bet your ass they're going to separate us."

"Why?" I ask, feeling another wave of unease wash over me. I hadn't realized how much comfort I've drawn from Minka's presence, and to think of that being taken away—well, it sucks. "Isn't it better for everyone if we're happy? We're less likely to cause problems, right?" I inwardly wince, knowing I sound like a hopeful Girl Scout.

Minka sighs, before releasing a small laugh. "You know what I love the most about you, Ni? You've always been too good for our world. No matter how much you've witnessed through the years, you never really saw it. Oh sure, you're aware of our way of life to a degree, but you've managed to keep it from tainting you. You're ever the optimist, and that's something I haven't been since I was a child—and maybe not even then. Please never let it change you." She ends on a whisper. And coming from my usually firecracker, ballbuster friend, that feels ominous.

We sit in silence. Finally, I ask, "Do you have a plan? I mean, if you knock the guards out, we could escape. But then what? A car blew up outside my home mere hours ago. Our only choice is to pick the lesser of the evils. And I haven't a clue who that is. My gut tells me that Marco won't hurt us." I shrug dejectedly. "That's just my opinion, which is probably clouded by the hot-guy factor."

Minka giggles, and a smile tugs at my own lips. Even in the worst of times, we've always been able to make each other laugh. "I've done a lot of stupid shit for worse reasons than that, so no judgment here." In the blink of an eye, she's serious once again, and it's beginning to freak me out. I'm not used to this solemn version of my best friend. "Please be careful. And no matter how much of a stud he is, don't trust Marco. It's not that I think he's totally evil, but he's mafia, Nina, and they live by a different code. I genuinely believe he likes you, but that matters little in his world. It's family first, and everything else last. Plus, I can't get past the *coincidental* timing. Franklin and his dipshit son are killed. Marco shows up at your place and then his car blows up. A few more Gavinos are taken out, and here we are."

"Marco feared the Gavinos would suspect me because of my link to Franklin," I say uncertainly. *Am I trying to convince her or myself that his intentions are pure?*

"So he decides to play the white knight to a woman he wants to bang? You two have never even held hands. Collateral damage is nothing to families like ours. Sure, it's unfortunate, but it happens." She clicks her tongue in the way she so often does when she's deep in thought. "There are only two reasons I can come up with. He either has genuine feelings for you, or he's guilty of something—and it's big."

"I'm sure he's got plenty of misdeeds on his conscience," I say ruefully. "I can't see any of them prompting him to stick his neck out for me."

"Even in our world, there's an honor of sorts. You saved his ass once, and this could be as simple as him settling that marker. If he's a decent guy, he's not going to want that hanging over his head. Unpaid markers are liabilities, and he will want to see it settled—especially if it involves an outsider. Your last name might be Gavino, but you're not one of us."

"Actually, it was Tony who promised me a marker when he came to collect Marco that night. He even gave me his card and told me to give him a call when I was ready to cash it in."

She whistles, looking impressed. "I can't believe you didn't tell me that. You have no idea how valuable it is. Hell, it's the equivalent of a blank check. I know of him enough to say he'll honor it. He's as big as they come—practically a king. That makes me feel a bit better about this mess. You have a valuable ace up your sleeve, and you're probably going to need it at some point. How do you think he'd feel about a buy-one-get-one-free arrangement?"

It takes a minute for her meaning to sink in. I can tell by the curve of her lips that she's joking, but I'm not when I say, "I will always have your back, Min. There's no way I'd save my own ass and leave you to fend for yourself. It's us against the world, same as it's been since the day we met."

"Ah yeah, that joyful moment when I drove my bony knee into my cousin's nuts. Even back then, I knew he had a lot of spare room in his tighty-whities." We both grimace as we ponder Frankie Jr.'s shortcomings. It's probably some inexcusable sin to think snide thoughts of the dead, but I'm not exactly broken up over his passing. "I can only imagine how scared you must have been to have not only a new family but also to have your stepbrother making a pass at you. I liked you instantly for giving me the opportunity to hurt the bastard. I swear he was nothing more than a human shit-stain."

"I kind of fell in love with you that day," I admit, not worried she'll take my words in a sexual way. Our friendship long ago transcended all normal barriers. We are soul mates and sisters in every way that matters. I am the only one in her life who knows the real Minka. The one who longs to spread her wings and fly. The gifted artist who dreams of breaking away from her family to chase her dreams. She tosses out so many decoys that even her own parents have no clue who she really is. She comes off as tough as nails— and that is accurate *superficially*. She could and would bring any man or woman to his or her knees without hesitation. But she is also sensitive, compassionate, generous, and loving. When my mother succumbed to cancer, Minka held me while I cried. She made certain I never spent a night alone in Franklin's house after that. She feared that Frankie would take advantage of the grief-induced daze that Franklin had been in and corner me. I owed her everything. She had my unspoken marker, and it was a debt that would never be paid in full.

I see the moisture in her eyes as she hugs me. "And I with you, kid," she jokes. She's barely a year older than me, but she told me once that I was likely to be the only child she ever had, and she intended to raise me right. Hence the "kid" reference.

We are so lost in the moment that we both jump when a voice says, "I've always been a sucker for girl-on-girl." Our heads turn as one to see

Nic leaning against the wall with Marco a few feet away wearing an unusually blank expression. "Please don't stop on our account." Nic shoots a disgusted look at his friend before adding, "Why didn't I keep my mouth shut?"

Marco shakes his head in exasperation. "You can't imagine how many times I've asked myself that very question."

"Showtime," Minka murmurs. "Go along with me on this, even if I sound insane." When my eyes widen, she adds, "It's for the best, Ni." Nic is the picture of leery when she jumps to her feet in one smooth motion. I've always been envious of the way she appears to almost glide while I'm lucky to walk through an empty room without tripping over my own feet. "So I assume this is where you split the prisoners up." Her nose curls as if she's smelled something particularly foul. "I guess I'm stuck with you, Nicole. I swear, why can't I ever get the hot one? All my guards are either related to me or fugly."

"Fugly?" he asks in confusion. "Papa Gavino wasn't big on education, I see. And the name is Nicoli as you're well aware."

"It means fucking ugly." I smile sweetly. "But that lingo is generally used by the younger, hipper crowd." *Take that, asshole. No one insults my friend and gets away with it.*

He shoots a disgusted look at Minka. "Your nastiness is wearing off on her."

She holds her hand out, and I bump my first against hers automatically. "She almost shot your dick off all on her own. If she'd had a rifle with a scope, then you'd have been in trouble, tiny."

"As amusing as this is," Marco interjects, "I'd like to get out of here sometime today. So if you two could delay the foreplay until you're alone, that would be great."

Minka was right. We're being separated. I open my mouth to object, but she shoots me a look. "Whatever." She shrugs, sounding bored. "Let's get going, Nicole. There's a new episode of *Walking Dead* on tonight. So unless you have a DVR set for it, I'm going to need you to get your ass in gear." She waves a hand in his face impatiently when he simply stands there. "Should I repeat myself? Maybe draw you a picture in crayon? And I'd like to stop at Arby's for some curly fries. I'm starving. The food we had earlier sucked ass."

The urge to laugh is so strong that I avert my head from the bemused expression both men are wearing. "I'm ready to go too." I motion to Marco. "This is Rick's final episode, and I don't want to miss a single minute of it." Turning to Minka, I ask, "How do you think they'll do it? I hope he doesn't get eaten. That would be so wrong after all these years."

Shaking her head, Minka says, "My money's on Daryl or Carol finally losing their shit and taking him out. That would be such a betrayal, though. I'd rather him end up as a zombie happy meal than for that to happen."

My stomach growls as she finishes her sentence. "Hey, can we stop by McDonald's? The McRib is back, and I've been dying for one."

Marco touches his flat stomach as if afraid that my words will undo all his hard work at the gym. He's probably one of those people who avoids carbs like they're the root of all that's evil. *Mmm, whatever he's doing, it's working. Yum. Stop! Have some pride. He's the enemy. But... he's so pretty. If he were on the menu, he'd be called The Big McMarco. Oh, brother.* "This isn't some kind of prep school sleepover," Nic says mockingly.

"Just get her the damn food," Marco grunts. "Kindness breeds kindness and all that other shit."

Nic stares at his friend as if he's grown two heads. "That was deeply moving, Mother Theresa. Before this gets any weirder, I'm going to escort this sweet young lady to Arby's and buy her all the curly fries she wants. Then we'll continue to our summer estate where we'll watch network television while she cleans her guns."

"Now you're speaking my language, Nicole." Minka winks. "If you keep this up, you might earn a good-behavior bang."

"Is that a threat?" He makes a show of gagging, but I don't miss the gleam of interest in his eyes. I'm fairly certain their barbs are a flimsy cover for what's really going on between them. And considering we usually tell each other everything, I'm a bit hurt she's been less than forthcoming about it. *What are you hiding, Min, and why?* I understood that a relationship between a Gavino and Moretti could be tricky. In the unlikely event that Marco and I became involved, I don't think it would be as much of an issue as I'm not a Gavino by blood. *But why wouldn't she tell me?* She certainly knows that I have the hots for Marco.

As Nic turns to speak to Marco, Minka pulls me in for one last hug. "Trust me. I have a plan—sort of. But I need to buy some time while I think it through. You'll be safe with Marco, but don't let your guard down. Something's not right here." She pulls away and moves to Marco's side. "You better take care of my little sister, Moretti. Because if anything happens to her, I'll hunt you down, cut your dick off, and feed it to you before I kill you."

"For fuck's sake, what is it with you Gavino women and your dick threats?" Nic chokes out. "I mean, can't all our body parts just get along?"

Marco smirks as he nods once at Minka. "I'll guard her with my life. I already have."

"Indeed." She smiles approvingly. Nic plows into her back when she stops suddenly in the doorway. "Oh, and make sure you wrap it up, kids. As much as I'd like to be Auntie Minka, we can't risk my girl catching something from that overused pecker of yours."

She did not just say that. I hear the departing couple bickering until their voices finally fade in the distance. "You ready to go?" Marco asks as he eyes me warily.

I cross to a table a few feet away and pick up my laptop bag, sliding the strap over my shoulder, followed by my purse. "I assume my suitcase is still in the car?"

"Nic will put it in the Escalade we'll be using." Unlike with Nic and Minka, there is complete silence between us as he follows me down the long corridor. He places a hand lightly on my lower back and guides me through a series of turns until we step out into the afternoon sunshine. Marco always has an unrelenting intensity about him, but I feel as though something has shifted. *There's no... heat. As if he's got me in his clutches but is no longer interested in taking what he wants. Wanted?* But I can't think about that now. *Stay alert, Nina.* I glance around me in interest as we walk toward the garage area where a fleet of black SUVs is parked behind a locked fence. The Moretti offices look a little different than most area corporate businesses. The building is a mixture of glass and steel with electronic gates at all entrances. But if you take a closer look, you'll notice the armed men who patrol the perimeter. They might rely on the latest technology as their first line of defense, but there is no shortage of good, old-fashioned muscle here. If somehow you made it past the gate, you wouldn't get far. Even Marco's hand has been scanned twice by the time we pull onto the road in the Escalade.

"That was like something straight out of the movies," I say dryly as he easily navigates the traffic congestion in the city.

"You should wipe all that from your memory, Belle. Pretend you've never been behind the walls."

"All right. Do you ever bring outsiders there?"

He grunts as if I've asked a stupid question. *Duh, it's a one-way trip for some of their guests.* Neither of us attempts to break the awkward silence that has fallen between us. For the first time since he showed up at my apartment, I wonder if I wouldn't have been better off fending for myself. I met him over a year ago, but we're not exactly friends. I have no clue why Minka and I trust him because we have nothing to base it on other than intuition—which has undoubtedly bitten both of us in the ass before. Sure, we've spent time together, but we haven't exactly been braiding each other's hair and sharing secrets. And he separated us, exactly as Minka had predicted. *Why?* I have a very unsettling feeling that I've stumbled into something I wasn't supposed to. Is his only motivation to protect me, or am I merely an unwitting pawn in a mafia game? Even if I could give him the benefit of the doubt due to the debt he owed me, what about his father? Sure, he's probably grateful I helped his son, but does that really matter to a man in his position? Not only am I a potential liability, but I'm also a Gavino—at least partly. And my best friend is the Gavino family princess. Mafia royalty like Tony. I'm not an idiot. That makes me a dangerous person to have around. If Marco believes the Gavinos want to get rid of me, then the Morettis have even more reason to see me gone. No one likes dealing with an unknown, but in this world, having that type of label could very well be a death sentence. Yesterday, I thought my biggest concern was whether or not my favorite coffee was still discounted at Starbucks. Now it's whether I'll live until my next birthday. And quite frankly, that just pisses me off. I dart my eyes in his direction, desperately wanting to see something—anything—to offer even a shred of reassurance that he's on my side. But as with most things in my life—there is no answer there. His honor as a man and that of Tony's are all I have to go on, and even though I may appear outwardly calm, I clutch those two invisible things to me with all I have. A part of me believes Marco will save me if possible, but if the time comes when he must decide between the family and me, then I'm as good as dead. Which is something I need to remind myself of every hour of the day. Any woman foolish enough to fall in love with a mafia man must accept that she'll always come last. If Marco means nothing to me, then why does that thought hurt so damn much?

4

Marco

"I'll admit, I thought you were kidding about the McRib thing." I shake my head as I stare at the tiny woman before me in amazement. Not only did she eat the supersized meal, but she also asked for extra barbecue sauce to dip her fries in as well as an apple pie for later. I'd been certain she couldn't possibly eat half the amount of food she ordered, but she passed that milestone several moments ago and shows no sign of stopping. When she wipes her mouth on her arm, I'm not sure if I'm disgusted or in love. Never have I met someone with so many quirks before. Usually when I'm with a woman, they do their best to appear as if they never eat, nor have a single hair out of place. Nina is either extremely comfortable in her own skin, or she just doesn't give a rat's ass about impressing me. Then a horrible thought occurs to me. *Fuck, have I fallen into the friend zone for the first time ever?* No, hell no. It can't be that. That's the land of no return. My cock jumps to a painful and full alert when she begins licking the sauce from her fingers. *Please God, I promise to be a better man—by maybe five percent if it's not true.* When the lick becomes a full-fledged sucking, sweat beads on my forehead.

All right, name your price. Whatever it takes. I can't be her brother or BFF. I want to fuck her too damn much for that.

Swear to Christ, she lets out a small burp, and I'm tempted to cry. I cast a desperate look upward in silent appeal. "That was so good," she moans blissfully. *So not helping, Belle.* "I have no idea why McDonald's doesn't offer the McRib year round. Everyone I know loves it."

I discreetly rearrange my cock, hoping she doesn't notice that the damn thing has lost its mind. "That's exactly why," I say distractedly. "A limited edition sells more in a short time than something that's readily available." I wrinkle my nose as I add, "Plus, there would be a major pig shortage in the world—if that's what it's even made of."

She gathers her trash and crosses my kitchen to the trash can. "Better people than you have tried to ruin the moment for me, Moretti, and I'm still one of the first in line when they come back. Thank God for Google alerts. You're probably one of those clean eaters. All organic and carbohydrate free." I walk over to my refrigerator and throw open the freezer. Inside are half a dozen containers of Ben and Jerry's in various flavors. She stares at me like I'm a superhero. *All those months of trying to win her over with my charm, and all it takes to impress her is Ben & Jerry's? Unbelievable.* "That's pretty hot," she murmurs reverently. I'm seconds away from making my move when she turns her back and tosses out, "*Walking Dead* in fifteen minutes. How about turning it on while I use the bathroom?"

Cold shower, anyone? I debate grabbing a pint of ice cream to hold against my crotch, but figure I'll lose major points for that. So between gritted teeth, I ask her retreating form, "Do you need me to show you where the bathroom is?"

"Nope, I took a tour while you were outside the door talking to your bodyguard." Then she has the audacity to pivot around and wiggle her eyebrows at me. "Guess all your men work out, huh? And what are the odds that there isn't an ugly one in the bunch? Is this Jake's regular post?" *She meets him for all of two seconds and remembers his name?* It galls me that she normally only calls me Moretti. *Probably because she can't remember YOUR name.* I instantly feel a wave of irritation toward my cousin. *Is this what jealousy feels like? If so, it fucking sucks. No. I am not jealous. That would be stupid.*

"No, it's not," I snap. "My much older cousin will be doing the honors tomorrow. He was sick today. Speaking of, they've all been passing around a stomach bug, so I'd steer clear of Jake. Just yesterday, he couldn't stop shitting long enough to drive to work." *Did I just resort to that?* Even I'm ashamed of my deceit. But I don't bother taking it back. *All's fair in love and war, right?* Or in our case, lust and mayhem. It may have been petty, but I'm pleased to see the disgusted expression on her face as she cringes.

"That's too bad. I'm sure he won't be contagious for long, though," she tosses out as she walks away. *Fuck. I should have said he was gay.* What does it even matter? I've never been insecure where a woman is concerned—the complete opposite in fact. I'm so busy trying to make sense of what I'm feeling that Jake is running through the front door a split second before the sound of a gunshot registers. And it's close by.

Nina.

"Bathroom," I hiss as I pull a handgun from my ankle holster. Jake calls for backup on his two-way radio then automatically steps in front of me—falling into the role of my human shield. Tony has always hated the fact that Nic and I do the same with him. And truthfully, I don't like it any more than he does. What gives us the right to determine that one human life is more valuable than another? It's a bit too much like playing God to me, but it's the way of the family and to object would offend those sworn to protect me. It's considered an honor by some to risk their lives for their superiors.

Within seconds, Jake has his shoulder against the door, sending it flying inward. I have no idea if it had even been locked, but the element of surprise is what's most important. We stand in the opening blinking rapidly as we attempt to process the scene before us. A man wearing black is lying on his back on the floor while Nina stands over him with her foot on his throat and a gun aimed at his crotch. *She seriously must hate that body part.* "I was sitting on the toilet when this dickhead stepped out of the linen closet and nearly gave me a heart attack. If my pistol hadn't still been in my bra, it would have been bad."

"I love you," Jake whispers under his breath, and I am seriously tempted to do the same fucking thing to him that Nina is doing to the bastard on the floor.

I shove past in disgust and squat down next to the intruder. I place my gun against his forehead and say with deadly calm, "Start talking, motherfucker."

His eyes are wide with terror as he whispers, "I think I made a huge mistake."

"That's an understatement," Jake snaps. "What you did, you stupid fucker, is sign your own death certificate." Jake cancels the backup he called for, seeing it's obviously nothing we can't handle.

I study the man on his back intently but don't detect even a faint resemblance to anyone in the Gavino organization. At one time or another, I've seen them all, and I don't know him, which is puzzling. But when he begins to sob, I'm downright confused. Even the biggest of pussies wouldn't dare cry in front of the enemy. No fucking way. What in the hell? "My mother is going to be so mad at me," he chokes out.

"Seriously?" Nina mutters in disgust before lowering her weapon. "It's rather pointless to threaten his manhood when he clearly doesn't possess it."

"He's not a Gavino," Jake says, echoing my own thoughts.

"I'm Langdon Foster," he sobs. "My mom, Sophie, is your cleaning lady. She's always talking about how rich you are and I—"

"You were planning to rob me." Then something occurs to me. "Who fired the shot?"

Nina raises her hand as if she's in school and has been called on by the teacher. "That would be me. He started for the door, and I didn't want to risk him catching you by surprise. So I took a warning shot." I follow her eyes as she looks upward at a gaping hole in my ceiling. "My bad," she says sheepishly.

"Fuck my life. Could you not have simply called out?"

She flushes in embarrassment, which I can't help but find rather endearing. "Er—I didn't think of that. Sorry."

I don't bother questioning the kid further about his identity. He's the spitting image of Sophie. It might have occurred to me earlier if I'd had any reason to suspect her offspring was hiding in my apartment. "Just how the hell did you get in here?" This place has been crawling with guards since the explosion, and it's fucking pathetic that this punk managed to sneak right past them. *So much for being safe in my own home.*

"I snuck in when my mom was here last. She had no clue," he adds quickly, obviously just realizing that his mother could be in trouble for his stupid actions.

"That was three days ago," I say skeptically. *For fuck's sake, don't say it.*

But in the next breath, he confirms my suspicions. "Yeah, I kind of hid in here, then waited for an opportunity to get out. But I hadn't counted on so many guys showing up and not leaving. I've been trapped." He gives me a thumbs-up that has me puzzled until he adds, "Dude, you're my hero. That blonde chick you had here the other night was smoking, and man, what a set of pipes she had on her. I hope this place is well insulated. Otherwise, all your neighbors know your business."

I blame Jake's laughter and Nina's death stare for my next actions. The little dumb fuck may not know it, but he has them to thank for the mercy he's about to receive. *Mainly, I want to get rid of his ass before he cockblocks me forever. Holy fucking hell.* The night I finally decide to relieve my months' worth of blue balls from hell—Nina does *not* want us to be a thing—this fucker happens. *Great timing, Moretti.* I motion for a still-fuming Nina to step back, then I pull Langdon to his feet by the collar of his hoodie. He squeaks in surprise, and I'm afraid he might piss himself, but he keeps it together. "Jake, take this kid home and tell his mother what he's been up to." Langdon's surprise is more like alarm now, which gives me a small glimmer of happiness. "If she's not home, then wait. He doesn't leave your sight until she's been brought up to speed on her halfwit's activities."

"Oh, come on, man. You know how my mom is. She'll take a stick to me for this." He squares his thin shoulders and looks me in the eyes. He might be a moron, but I give him credit for bravery, even if he has no clue who he's dealing with. If he did, he'd realize his mama is by far the lesser of two evils here. "I ain't got nothing of yours on me. I gave up on stealing when I realized I'd be lucky to get out of here myself, much less take anything with me." He raises his hands in the air. "Go ahead and check me over."

I roll my eyes, then give him my best bored look. I even toss in a yawn for good measure. "Jake wouldn't have let you in the car without patting you down, kid. This isn't amateur hour."

"Don't you need to check me for a weapon?" he asks in confusion. "I could be packing and waiting for an opportunity."

"You're not that fucking brave or intelligent," I scoff. "Plus, if you had any options, you wouldn't have been lying on the floor like a pussy while Nina wiped her feet all over you. Now, man the fuck up and take your punishment. Then thank whoever it is you believe in for the fact that you're leaving alive."

But the kid will not shut the fuck up. "I want to make this right, Mr. Moretti. I know you're gonna tell my ma, and she'll be really pissed at me. Probably throw me out again. But I owe you for taking it easy on me after I disrespected you and your property. I went through all your things, and I listened to you and that woman—"

"Stop!" *Is he suicidal or insane?* Being friend-zoned by Nina is probably the best of outcomes at this point. I'll be lucky if she doesn't neuter me with her gun after this wealth of oversharing. "Trust me, kid, you'll pay the marker you owe me and more." I can't believe the words out of my mouth, and by the shocked expressions Nina and Jake are wearing, they're just as surprised. I go to my Zen place as I smirk at my cousin. He knows me well enough to be wary of my sudden change of mood. "You'll be working for Jake until further notice. If he wants you to lick the vehicles clean, scrub the toilets, or untie and retie his fucking boots all day, you'll do it. If he tells me even once that you're doing anything other than what you're supposed to be doing, you won't like what happens."

He's ashen by the end of my speech, but there's also a sense of pride about him that hadn't been there before. I know Sophie's a single mother and there isn't a man in the picture. I'm curious and make a mental note to get the full story. I'm sure there's a file at the office containing everything I need. Outsiders aren't allowed access to the family without being vetted. "You won't be sorry, Mr. Moretti. You'll see. I'm a good worker. I just made a mistake." He puts his hands in his pockets and shuffles uneasily on his feet. "These guys said I owe them money, and if I don't pay, then my sister's gotta work it off." His eyes are moist when he adds quickly, "I swear, I don't owe them nothing. They're pissed because I won't join their crew. But I promised my mama I wouldn't do the shit my cousin Travis did, ya know?"

So much for the brief moment of happiness. Fuck. I'm beginning to feel like the patron saint of lost and endangered souls. I should fire Sophie and wash my hands of this whole fucking mess. *Shoulda, coulda, and fucking didn't.* Jake's eyes are narrowed, and I know he doesn't like what he's heard any more than I do. We might be mafia, but we don't prey upon kids. "I'll handle it," he grunts. We don't leave loose ends. Sloppiness will get you killed—or make you wish you were dead. Not to say there haven't been some less than motivated Morettis at times, but that's usually a mistake only made once. There is no employee file with written warnings and the three-strike method. We can't afford to be lenient with those who hold the lives of many others in their hands, and that point is driven home to every new family member. They need to understand that if their carelessness causes the death of another, then the same will be visited upon them. Is it brutal? Sure, but the real world operates in much the same way. If you're in the military and you fuck up your assignment, then you may as well put a gun to another soldier's head and pull the trigger. No matter what field you're in, the domino effect is always in play; the only things that differ are the stakes.

The tips of Langdon's ears are blood red when he nods sheepishly to Nina. "Sorry about scaring you. I swear I didn't see nothing but... maybe your black panties. And that was only because they were around your ankles."

I need a drink—no a bottle. Just when I think this kid couldn't possibly be any dumber, he opens his mouth, and more stupidity spills out. I wait in silence, figuring Nina will teach him a much-needed lesson. But to my shock, she begins laughing. After staring daggers at me for the past five minutes over my... extracurricular activities, she grins fondly at Langdon as if he's an adorable puppy. If that's not bad enough, she goes right up to the little asshole and throws her arms around him. *The fuck is this?* "It's all good, dork. And I hope your throat's all right." She pulls back to examine the area in question, and I seriously consider pounding my head against the wall to see if this whole thing is a dream. "Now, you listen to what Jake says and don't get into trouble. I'm proud of you for taking responsibility for your actions. It takes a man to admit they've made a mistake and to genuinely want to make restitution." *What the actual fuck? Nina in mother-bear mode?* She waves a hand in our direction before adding, "And I know that took a lot of courage considering what you've probably heard about er... the Morettis. I don't know Jake, but I can vouch for Marco." For a split second, I have that elusive warm, fuzzy feeling before she tacks on, "But please don't go idolizing him. Find yourself a nice girl who respects herself and you."

His head bobs up and down as he flashes her a look of puppy love. I'd find it rather sweet if the kid hadn't fed me to the dogs with his loose lips. "I will, Miss Nina." And once again, I'm almost rid of my interloper when he leans down to whisper loud enough for his mother across town to hear, "He doesn't have a daughter, does he?" *Well, that is plain baffling.* We're all mentally scratching our head at his farfetched question when he nicely decides to elaborate. "That blonde lady said she'd been a bad girl and needed a spanking."

Oh fuck.

"Langdon," I say in a voice that should have dropped him on the spot, but he's like a goddamn wrecking ball, and I'm the building he's intent on toppling. Jake is holding his sides and gasping for breath, while waves of disgust are rolling off Nina like waves crashing on the shore.

"I wouldn't think much of it if she hadn't kept calling him Big Daddy. Seemed like a funny nickname for what they were doing and all."

Nina appears to comprehend that her newfound puppy is in grave peril because she clasps his arm firmly and propels him in Jake's direction. "Langdon's mother is probably worried about him. He needs to go home now."

Jake seems disappointed the show is over, but he gathers his composure and motions Langdon ahead of him. He pauses long enough to say, "Security system is still updating." He hands me a slip of paper, before adding, "There's the new code. Should be ready to set as usual in another thirty." He moves in Langdon's direction, and I hear the kid chatting aimlessly, but thankfully, I can't make his words out. I shudder to think what other fun facts he's filling my cousin's head with. I'll never live this shit down. *I'll have to kill Jake to keep this from getting out.* I brace myself for Nina's attack, but she brushes past me and leaves the bathroom. Whoever said silence was golden had obviously never encountered a quiet woman. I've always felt it better to get problems out in the open, rather than let them fester into something uglier. But women like to "process." Which is code for, striking when you least expect it. They run through every possible scenario and figure out ways to neatly box you in so you have no choice but to wave the white flag and beg for mercy. Hell, I'd be tempted to toss out a few tears right now if she'd let this go. *Dare to dream.* Even though it's the last thing I want to do, I move through my home until I find her in the kitchen standing in front of the microwave. She opens the door and tosses a bag of popcorn inside. A chill runs down my spine as she whistles while waiting for her snack. "How can you possibly be hungry after eating that much food an hour ago?" *Oh, shit. Rookie mistake, Moretti.* I know better than to question a woman's eating habits, especially one who's already pissed at me. Clearly, I'm not of sound mind right now.

"It's for *Walking Dead*. I always have a snack when I'm watching it." She cuts her eyes at me in a way that makes me want to crawl from the kitchen. "If seeing a woman eat is too nauseating for you, then feel free to go elsewhere." She empties the bag into a nearby bowl and finds the bottle of movie theater butter in the cabinet. I applaud myself for keeping a straight face while she saturates the popcorn until it glistens. I have a feeling that part of it is for my benefit, but I wisely avert my gaze and zip my lips.

When she picks up her snack and turns toward the living room, I open the refrigerator and grab a beer. "What would you like to drink?" There's no fucking way I'll take her a glass of water or a diet soft drink at this point even though most women I know seem to prefer those two things.

I know I was right to wait when she calls out, "Coke. Regular, if you have it." She's sitting cross-legged on my leather sofa while she flips through the channels on my remote. Her brow is furrowed as her finger frantically pushes the channel up button. "Oh my God, Moretti, where is AMC? I swear if Rick dies in the first part of the show, I'm going to lose it." She drags a hand through her hair, leaving a piece sticking comically up. *I think that ship has already sailed, Belle.*

Risking bodily harm, I pluck the remote from her grasp and bring up the guide. Within a few moments, she's happily munching on her snack while I'm staring at the television in revulsion. *How can she eat during this? I want to fucking puke.* This is the goriest show I've ever watched. Give me *The Sopranos* any day. Seeing some dude torture another is far easier to stomach than a zombie eating some guy's arm off. "So this is your favorite show, huh? Isn't this a bit... unsettling?"

She completely ignores my question as her attention remains riveted on the carnage unfolding in all its high-definition glory. It's one of the few times I wish I didn't have a television. At least fifteen minutes pass before she responds to my questions as if I've just asked them. "Minka and I have watched this since the beginning. Normally, we'd either be together or at least texting each other during it." She shoots me a dirty look that plainly says, *thanks for ruining it, asshole.* I almost point out that no one has taken her cell phone away, but I'd rather not open that can of worms tonight. This is a tricky situation that even I'm not sure how to explain. Neither are technically our prisoners—nor are they free to go. The official story is they're under our protection. If Nina should refuse that, then this will get much more difficult. I am concerned for her safety—that much is true—as is the fact that she's at risk right now with the unrest in our world. What she doesn't know is that she's sitting mere inches away from the man who may have very well painted a target on her back.

"This doesn't seem like your kind of thing," I say, attempting to get her off the subject of Minka.

"There are more things in life than the Playboy Channel, Moretti." She smirks, then goes back to ignoring me when the commercial break is over.

Despite myself, I'm thoroughly engrossed in the violent drama by the time it ends. I stare at the screen in bewilderment, thinking I must have missed something. "Where the hell did they take Rick? I thought you said he was going to die, but he's clearly alive in the helicopter." Instead of a response, I hear a sniffle. *Really? Swear to fuck, I refuse to be jealous of a television character.* Exasperated and more than a little tired, I grumble, "Belle, this isn't real. The dude is an actor who makes a shitload of money to wear a nasty, sweat-stained shirt every week. He's somewhere safe and sound having a beer and hoping they'll turn this crap into a movie." I feel like the world's biggest jerk when her sniffles turn into full-blown sobs. I've never been good with tears, and Nina has been on an emotional roller coaster since learning of Franklin's death. I reach out and awkwardly pat her knee, attempting to offer her comfort that says without actually saying, *sorry I killed your family earlier.* Greeting card companies would clean up if they expanded their selection of sympathy cards.

Her mascara has smeared so much that she resembles a raccoon when she stares at me. "Why does everything I love go away, Marco? Am I cursed?"

Oh fuck. Go ahead and take me now, Lord. Put me out of my misery. I'm still struggling to find the right words when she shocks the hell out of me by getting on her knees and crawling in my lap. God, it seems, has a wicked sense of humor. "Belle," I murmur helplessly. "Rick is still alive. I know you love the show, and this sort of thing can be kinda... hard to handle, but he didn't get eaten by a zombie, so there's still hope, baby." I wince at the intimacy of the endearment I've used, but she doesn't appear to have noticed.

Instead of helping, I seem to be doing the opposite. My poor shirt is taking the brunt of the damage. It's like trying to use a Kleenex to mop up the Hoover Dam. I'll take the wet shirt any day, though, over the damp nose she has pressed into the side of my neck now. "It's not just that," she hiccups, and I pat her back as if I'm trying to burp an infant. Hell, I have no clue what to do with a hysterical woman. Usually, when they lose it around me, they throw shit and use "fuck" a lot. What now? Maybe a glass of water—or vodka? *Bottle of Valium?* I'm seriously considering texting my mom for advice when she begins speaking again. Crap, she was waiting for me to ask her what else she is upset over. *But... I don't want to know.* "First, there was my dad and then my mom." *Wait—is her father dead?* Fuck, I have no clue. Better to remain quiet and hope she falls asleep. *Or I could send one of the guys for more food. That seems to make her happy.* "And even though I was conflicted over his way of life, I loved Franklin. And now he's gone. Frankie was a turd, and I didn't like him at all." I'm nodding, in full agreement on that last statement when she slaps her hand over her mouth so loudly that I wince. *Damn, that must have hurt.* Her bottom lip is wobbling as she says tearfully, "I'm going to hell now, right? It's a sin to speak badly of the dead."

"You get a pass when the recently deceased is a worthless twat," I say confidently. *Let's hope that extends to those who exterminate said twats from the earth.*

She blinks rapidly, and I can almost see her brain processing my words. Even if she calls bullshit, at least it's stopped the crying for the moment. I'm silently congratulating myself on talking her from the ledge when the tears return—*again.* Fuck me, how long has this been going on? Shouldn't she have run out of moisture by now? She nods in the direction of the kitchen as if I'm able to read her mind. *More popcorn?* Maybe she's an emotional eater. "Then there's the McRib. Another thing that leaves me again and again. I smile and welcome it into my life, but it doesn't really care about my feelings, ya know? It disappears with no warning, and I'm left to wonder why."

This has got to be a joke. I expect to see Jake and Langdon pop out of a nearby closet at any moment laughing their asses off. I'll probably kill them, so I hope it's worth it. I shoot her a grave look as if I'm on board with this madness. "Yeah, that one sucks the most, Belle. Fuck the Big Mac. That's like winning runner-up in a beauty pageant.

They pat your head and tell you how pretty you are, but you know different. If you were all that, you wouldn't be standing on the sidelines while the hot chick walked off with the crown. Why not call a spade a spade, am I right? If you're not a winner, you're a loser. If you're not a McRib, you're a fucking burger." *That was kind of brilliant if I must say so.*

Her eyes are so wide they're damn near crossing. She hasn't blinked in at least a minute, and it's beginning to freak me out slightly. "I… guess so," she says carefully. Then she snaps her fingers, and my balls want to pack up and run. "What about Rick Grimes?"

"Who in the hell is that?" I mutter before dropping my head in defeat. "We aren't back to *Walking Dead,* are we? For the love of—Belle, it's not real. Do you lose it every time the zombies go all buffet on some poor bastard?" When she shakes her head, I grip her shoulders gently but firmly. "Then why are you so… emotional over tonight's episode? The dude didn't even die. From what little I saw, he's better off than the rest of them. You should be pissed that poor Molly and Darin are left riding horses and shooting a bow while he's on his way back to the land of WiFi and Prozac."

Something that sounds suspiciously like a giggle escapes her throat. "It's Maggie and Daryl." She snorts. "And where did the Prozac thing come from? I can think of many more important items than that."

"Are you serious? In a fucked-up world like that, a good anti-depressant would be priceless. The ability to go to your happy place while your best friend is zombie kibble, what could be better? Granted, an argument could be made for Jack Daniel's, but you could easily blow through that in a night. Better to have something on hand for the long term."

She crosses her arms over her chest and glares at me. *What now?* I'm seriously getting whiplash from these rapid-fire mood changes. Happy, sad, pissed, confused, and deranged. And that's just in the past half hour. I'm worn the fuck out. *I was joking about the Prozac, but that might not be such a bad idea.* "Based on what I know about you, Moretti, I would have guessed that you'd find a tramp to ease your suffering and not a pill. Well, unless it was Viagra. No judgment," she adds quickly.

"All men have performance problems from time to time. There's no shame in seeking medical attention."

She did not go there. Both my dick and I are outraged. Question anything except my ability to perform in all circumstances—for however long I desire. She's giving me an angelic smile that says she meant no offense, but I call bullshit. The little minx knew exactly what she was doing. Yet even knowing she's pulling my chain, I still can't help but take the bait. "I'll have you know, Belle, that I've never needed help in that area." I clamp my hands around her thighs and pull her snugly against the bulge in my pants. "I could fuck you right now until you couldn't remember your name, and I'd just be getting started. Every time you moved the next day, you'd be reminded of the feel of my cock slamming inside you." Her grin slides away as her breath catches in her throat. I'm smugly satisfied at turning the tables until I notice her nipples have hardened as they press against the material of her shirt. And that's not the only thing that's come to life. My cock is thrilled to discover that only a few layers of clothing separate us. I know I shouldn't... She's vulnerable, and only an asshole would take advantage of the situation we're in now, but fuck I've wanted her for so long. *Just one little taste of heaven before I return to hell...*

It all begins innocently enough, a simple slide of my lips against hers—almost chaste. A gentle tracing of her mouth with the tip of my tongue. *See, no problem. I'm in complete control—until I'm not.* This is where things get fuzzy. One moment, I'm pressing teasing kisses against that beautiful pout, and the next, she's captured my tongue and is sucking it into her mouth. This is where I officially lose it and turn into a fumbling schoolboy instead of a skilled lover. My only consolation is that she appears just as frantic as I am. My hands are everywhere at once as I attempt to touch every glorious inch I've previously been denied. I finally settle for gripping her ass and squeezing it. Not original in the least, but it feels so damn good. I'm not sure who's responsible, but her shirt has been pulled up and her bra down. *Wait—did she do that or did I? Who in the fuck cares?* There's a nipple near my mouth, and I don't waste another second trying to figure out how it got there. Her back arches, and she cries out as my teeth nip the dusky tip, then I soothe the sting with a flick of my tongue. Holy hell, she tastes amazing, like a ripe peach dipped in bourbon. An odd combination to compare a woman to, but that's exactly what Nina is to me—sweet and intoxicating. "Marco," she moans, and I damn near come in my pants. *Why is everything about this woman so sexy?*

I've unbuttoned her jeans, and my hand is halfway to nirvana when my phone rings.

Ignore it. They'll go away.

She lifts herself slightly, and I make it another inch before my two-way radio sounds.

Someone is dead.

I want to ignore it—fuck, do I ever—but that would be utterly foolish. "Goddammit," I hiss as Nina looks up at me with eyes full of desire. *If you hurry, you can pick right up...* But I know that's not going to happen. It's like she transforms into Nina Gavino, ice queen in seconds. *No vulnerable looks. No sex-crazed gaze. Shuttered expression.* Which means, of course, she's already pulling away. *The universe fucking hates me.* I click the intercom button on the radio and snarl, "WHAT?"

There's a moment of silence on the other end. I rarely lose my cool, so obviously I've taken whoever the hell it is by surprise. I didn't bother to look at the display before responding. Knowing my luck, it's probably my mother. "Marco." The grim tone in Jake's voice effectively cuts through my pity-party. *Something's very wrong.* "I took the kid home and —fuck, man, his family's dead. Mother took a shot to the head and chest. Sister had three rounds in her. Forehead, leg, and gut. I went in with the kid to give an explanation about his new job and— goddammit, what a fucking mess. I got the kid out of there and wiped my prints. Hell, I didn't know how you wanted to handle it."

Most things in my world require tactful concealment. I'm not worried that Nina will call the police, but I wish I had spared her the details. Had I not been so distracted, the gruesome picture Jake just described wouldn't have been another trauma Nina was subjected to. She's sitting in the corner of my sofa now with that same blank expression she was wearing earlier. She's retreated to that place we all go to when we can't handle anything more. "If you're certain you left nothing behind, then take the boy to the office and give him some time to decompress. The police will want to question him. As bad as I hate it, he really needs to be the one to give them a heads-up. Gonna look suspicious if he doesn't officially find them and follow the usual procedure."

"I agree." Jake sighs. "Maybe Rutger can talk to his contact and ease the way a bit. Kid's been in your apartment for days. Not that we want the scrutiny of being his alibi, but he couldn't have done it. Well, I suppose he could have left and come back, but that's unlikely. Someone would have seen him. Plus, they were killed today." He pauses for a moment, and I can almost see him swallowing hard before he adds, "It was... still fresh." I dart my eyes in Nina's direction and note that she doesn't appear to have moved an inch. Hell, her shirt is still pushed up on one side. As beautiful and desirable as she looks, sex is not even remotely on my mind. *Not with this.*

"Hey listen, let me think this through, and I'll hit you up in a few." I toss the radio aside and lean forward, rubbing absently at the tight knot in the back of my neck. *Mother took a shot to the head and chest. Sister had three rounds in her. Forehead, leg, and gut.* Fuck, it was a hit. Why Sophie? Related to me or some stupid shit of Langdon's? *Fuck. Sophie. What the fuck is going on?*

"Who killed them, Marco?" she asks in a voice as vacant as her expression. Her ability to disassociate herself from reality is unnerving. It makes me wonder what kind of shit has gone down in her life for her to perfect that kind of defense mechanism. Few are born with such skill. It takes trauma to hone it to the point that she has.

"I don't know, Belle," I reply honestly. And even though I have shit to handle, I pull her back against my chest and give us both the comfort we need. She's stiff at first, but she gradually relaxes as I absently drop a kiss onto the top of her head, while rubbing her back soothingly.

"It can't be a coincidence," she says, echoing my thoughts. "But why them? They're not connected to either of our families other than working for you, right?"

"Correct." I don't elaborate because this isn't a conversation we should be having. Nina already knows far too much and not only would the Gavinos frown on her involvement, but my family wouldn't like it either. You don't bring outsiders to dinner without an invitation, and you damn sure don't give a member of another family an all-access pass to your business. That's a diplomatic way of saying, trust no one, especially mafia. *She knows too much.* I might have had mostly good reasons for protecting her, but I'm beginning to think she'd have been better off on her own. I can only shield her so much from what's going on—unless I hand her off to someone much further down the food chain than me. My feelings for her are already interfering with my job and also my judgment. I'm making all kinds of excuses to justify her staying with me, when none are valid now.

"So what's the next move? Do we talk to Langdon and see what he knows or maybe check it out ourselves before the police become involved?"

I untangle her from my arms and get to my feet. I have to put some distance between us, so I can return to the asshole she's always accusing me of being. That guy can handle hurting her feelings. The man who only moments ago had his tongue in her mouth cannot. "We don't have a move, Nina. You're currently under our protection—that's it. I can no more discuss family business with you than I can Langdon or my barber. It's regrettable that you heard my conversation with Jake. It was an oversight on my part and not an attempt to include you in our operations." *Please don't fucking cry.* Her eyes are ablaze with anger—but her lips are trembling. I sound like an obnoxious prick, but I have to get my point across to her. *I'm trying to save your life, Belle.* The muscle in my cheek clenches as I await the explosion that never comes. Instead, she stands without uttering a word and walks away. Seconds later, I hear the bedroom door quietly close and then there's nothing. Her silence is more effective than a hard kick to the balls. And no doubt she knows that too. *But what is she thinking? No, Moretti, don't go there.*

How could there possibly be any happy marriages in our world? I'm not naïve. There must be some pillow talk going on. The Moretti women are not clueless. They knew what they were signing on for before they took their vows. There's also some who would enjoy looking like a big shot by bragging to their significant other. And there are undoubtedly wives who get tired of being kept in the dark and begin asking questions and snooping around. It's understandable on both accounts. It's against human nature to bind yourself to someone, yet keep a big chunk of your life from him or her. Sex and/or relationships are seldom simple. And it's doubly complicated for me. Fuck, if I mess up and talk in my sleep with the wrong person around, things could get ugly in a hurry. I wish I were a normal man who could follow Nina with my tail tucked between my legs and beg for forgiveness, but that's not going to happen. Instead, I shoot Jake a text and fix myself a cup of coffee while I wait for him. It's gonna be a long night, and it has little to do with Sophie's family and everything to do with the woman down the hall. For a moment, she was mine, and she tasted every bit as sweet as I expected.

But now I know she'll never be mine.

Fuck.

Nina

I flop onto Marco's big king-sized bed, feeling pathetically sorry for myself. I'm reeling from his words to me. It wasn't so much what he said, but the cold way he delivered the smackdown. I'm not sure why it was such a surprise, all things considered, but I hadn't expected it after what had happened between us. Which was a damn joke. The man fucked everything that moved. He was quite experienced at keeping his personal and professional life separated. His bimbos probably don't think unless he allows it. *Don't knock them, sweetheart, you were on your way to joining their ranks.* And that thought is more humiliating than anything. The first moment we're alone, and I toss my morals right out the window to hump his lap like a bitch in heat. How am I any better than the blonde that so impressed Langdon? Another chick whose panties magically fell away when Marco Moretti turned on the charm. Maybe this is what happens when you write romance novels for a living. Eventually, you look for hot make-out sessions and believe it means something. *But it's Marco, and I know there has been no pining for me on his end.*

I need to hash this out with Minka. She'll remind me to stay clear of Marco. I lift my head and look around until I spot my purse a few feet away. I crawl over to it and dig my phone from the side pocket. I'm still surprised Marco hasn't confiscated it yet. I don't want to risk calling her and alerting Nic. I can only hope he hasn't already taken hers. I send her a text in our own unique code and anxiously await a reply. *Where is she?* I yawn and wearily put the phone on vibrate and then lay it against my chest, so I'll know when she responds.

In the meantime, my thoughts drift over the events of the day, and I feel a pang in my heart. *Franklin is dead.* I still can't quite believe it. He's always been larger than life to me. Invincible. He was no longer a young man, but still—how could he have let someone kill him? There's something so human about that. Not sure what I was expecting, but he was mafia. I would have been less surprised by a car bomb, the kind that blew Marco's car to pieces. Now that was the type of mob stuff you see on television. I know it's wrong of me, but if Franklin had to die, then I'm absurdly glad that Frankie Jr. went out with him. My future would be scary indeed if he were alive and unchecked by his father. Although Franklin could be somewhat blind to his son's *many* faults, he wasn't stupid, by any means. And Frankie was careful about crossing big lines that he knew his father would disapprove of, which afforded me a small amount of protection. Well, that and the fact that Minka scared the hell out of him. She'd always known he was a snake, and it hadn't taken her long to understand that he couldn't be trusted where I was concerned. She's always brushed aside my gratitude, but we both know that our friendship has had many far-reaching implications and that may well be the most important one.

I like to think that my mom sent Minka to me to make up in some small way for leaving me behind. I realize it's childish and utterly pointless to blame someone for dying—it wasn't as if cancer was optional—but she postponed going to the doctor until it was too late. If only she'd gone earlier, then maybe she'd still be alive. She admitted toward the end that there had been a sense of foreboding. She'd known that the stomach pain she was feeling was more than one of the simple ulcers she'd had before. But she wanted to believe that if she ignored it, then it would go away. So that's what she did.

And to make matters worse, she assured Franklin she had seen a doctor, and it was nothing. The only one not blindsided by the news that she had stage 4 pancreatic cancer was her. It's one of the few times I can remember her arguing with Franklin. He'd been so angry, accusing her of recklessly throwing not only her life away, but his and mine as well. Of course, the next day, he hired the best doctors available. But as so many have learned, money can do many things, but it cannot buy you a cure when none exists. She squandered all her options by disregarding the warning signs. *By being afraid.*

I sometimes wonder if she did it on purpose. I do believe Franklin made her happy in a way and that she loved him, but a part of her never got over my father, her high school sweetheart and the love of her life. He was killed in a hunting accident, mistaken for a deer. According to her, he never knew she was pregnant. And unfortunately, she'd been raised by a single mother who had no desire to raise another child and certainly didn't want to be a grandmother. So after she had me, she relied on help from the state until she could find a job and a place to live. I hadn't been old enough then to understand how tough things must have been for her, but she never once made me feel as if I was a burden. Our apartment was small, but we always had what we needed. As I got older, I knew other kids dressed better than I did, and their parents had nicer cars, but I never cared. Thanks to the very kind man who owned the restaurant where she was a waitress, she was able to work a flexible schedule that allowed her to attend all my school functions and field trips. People seemed to gravitate to her since she was not only pretty but outgoing as well. I'd been so proud to have her as my mom. *And my biggest supporter. Which also meant I missed her so very much.*

Then Franklin Gavino walked into the restaurant, and it felt as if our lives changed overnight. He lavished her with nice things she'd never been able to afford, but more importantly, he gave her his time and attention. He made her feel as if she mattered, which was something she hadn't felt in a long time—if ever. I was ten when they were married in a small service at Franklin's home. My surname was changed along with my mother's to Gavino. It hadn't seemed like a big deal to me at the time. Heck, other than being jealous of sharing my mom, I was excited over our new adventure, as she liked to call it. But like every fairy tale, there had to be an evil turd—and that was where Frankie Jr. came in. He played the part of adoring brother when our parents were around, but when we were alone, he scared the hell out of me. Since he was bigger, he liked to bully me, then called me clumsy as if I tripped on my own rather than him pushing me. If that had been his only sin, I could have lived with it. But something in the way he looked at me set alarm bells off—loudly. *Thank God, he's gone.*

I don't know if he witnessed something I wasn't aware of, but Franklin appeared to be of a similar mind where his son was concerned, and he tried to ensure we weren't left alone in the house. Sadly, he'd been more observant than my own mother, who brushed aside all negative comments I made about Frankie. I think she was terrified of accepting it as the truth because it would mean her perfect new life wasn't all that it seemed. And worse yet, she would have to take action. I know my mother loved me dearly, so I can only conclude that things must have been much harder for her than I realized before Franklin came along. That's the only reason that makes any sense to me. *I need to believe that desperately.*

That's why Minka had been such a hero to me. We met at a family gathering, and she took me under her wing as if we'd always been friends. Unlike some of the others, she hadn't acted as if I didn't belong because I wasn't Gavino by blood. Hell, she mentioned more than once how envious she was of that very fact. She knew I had more freedom that she ever would. Her name made her a prisoner whereas, for me, it was more like loose shackles. Kind of like when celebrities receive a key to their home cities or an honorary degree from a university. It was simply for show and little else. In our case, it was Franklin's attempt to make us into a normal family—something I had to commend him for. Even as I cursed him for putting me in the position I now found myself in. That was primarily how I viewed my relationship with my stepfa-ther. Mostly a curse, but with a few sweet moments thrown in for variety. At least he tried. Oh, how I hated that voice in my head at times. The nasty bitch never failed to point out my shortcomings. I have no idea why, but it certainly liked Franklin better than me. And Marco too, for that matter.

Traitor.

And now I have no family left... and can admit I feel very alone.

Exhausted both mentally and physically, I snuggle into the soft comfort of Marco's bed and try not to think of all the germs probably crawling atop his 5000 thread count sheets. If I remain on top of the comforter, I should be fine. It's absurd, but I roll my eyes at myself and push everything else away. The necessity of staying here. The car bomb. Langdon and his family. Marco—especially—and my stupid lusting for a man as deep as a paper cut. No, it was time to tune out, take a nap, and hope that Minka has an answer. She always does. *God help us both if the day comes when she draws a blank.*

5

Marco

"Considering she hasn't spoken to me directly for a week, I'd say chances are strong she's still pissed off," I mutter in disgust. After my not-so-wonderful handling of her desire to help with the Langdon situation, I'd become public enemy number one. Fuck no. That would be a step up. I'm now the invisible man where she's concerned. I was happy to leave her at my place with a couple of men while I met Nic and Jake at the office. With no new leads on who killed the kid's family, I had Jake pull the security footage for my apartment on the outside chance someone followed either Langdon or Sophie when they'd been there. That kind of murder is rarely ever random. We just have to find the link.

I'm tempted to pull my gun on Nic when he chuckles at my predicament with Nina. "Still striking out even though you have the home-field advantage. Bro, that's just embarrassing. I figured you two would have given in to temptation long ago."

The image of Nina sitting on my lap while I sucked her tits floats through my head, and I begin recounting baseball statistics under my breath to keep my body from responding. *I fucked up royally. No one to blame but myself.* "She hasn't addressed me directly since I fucked up. If Jake's there, she says something like, 'Jake, tell Mr. Moretti that he is out of Coke,' or she leaves me a note." I pull a piece of paper from my pocket and hand it to him. He unfolds it, and his eyes scan the page before he bursts into laughter.

"Damn," he gasps out. "I hope you took that shit seriously. Plus, it's gotta be some comfort that you wouldn't be seeing any action right now regardless."

"What's it say?" Jake asks as he attempts to look over Nic's shoulder. *"Mr. Moretti, unless you want your no doubt outrageously expensive brothel bed ruined, I advise you to pick up a box of heavy flow tampons ASAP. Doesn't really matter much to me either way. Ms. Nina Gavino."* Jake and Nic sag against the wall, not even trying to contain their amusement. *Surely, my father would understand if I shot one of them. He'd never put up with this.*

"Laugh it up, ladies," I say in a voice so quiet and calm, they're immediately on alert. They've been around me long enough to know when to be wary. "I'm glad you two can find such humor in my problems when we have so many bigger things to focus on. But if you feel that this is a priority, then take all the time you need." Looking the picture of tolerance, I sit down in a nearby chair and cross my legs, whistling casually. *Keep a straight face. This is too good to ruin now.*

Nic gives me a skeptical stare before shaking his head. "Dude, I think Jake may have shit his pants. For fuck's sake, tell him you're kidding." My other cousin is a bit pale, and considering I need him right now, it's best to put him out of his misery.

I roll my eyes in his direction. "Stop being such a pussy. If you have an accident in here, I'll make sure everyone sees it. Including Tony and Lee."

He's already shaking his head frantically. "Don't you dare tell them such bullshit. What in the hell is wrong with all of you?" he grumbles under his breath as he turns back to the video monitor. "If you don't eat your young and knock your woman around, you're a pussy. Something fucked about that."

"Hey, hey." Nic chuckles as he slaps the other man on the back of the head. "You have us confused with the Gavinos. You know the big man made that rule about laying hands on a chick. Said he'd let his wife personally deliver the punishment if he found out anyone broke the rule. And no one wants Mama Moretti on them." He shudders. "There are no written laws about munching on your kids, but I don't think that's ever come up before. You're into some weird shit, dude. But I still love you."

It's damn near impossible to be in the same room with these two and not be amused at the insane conversations they have. To an outsider, they'd be deemed certifiable. *Might not be too far off.* But there's no one else I'd rather work with than them.

Then how could you betray their trust?

The sick feeling is back in the pit of my stomach. Feels like I've swallowed broken glass and washed it down with battery acid. *Please let them never know I was involved.* I realize my mood is somber in part because of the rift with Nina, but toss in the fact there's a kid down the hall still reeling from finding his mother and sister murdered, and it makes me wonder how bad things would have to get for us to go through a day without joking around. *I know one thing that would do it.* "Fuck you, asshole," Jake mutters before glancing over at me warily. "How far back you want to go again, boss? I got like thirty days of footage here, but that's gonna take a while to go through."

I pull out my phone and bring up my calendar. "Sophie would have been there on Monday. So let's cover our bases and start on Sunday. See if anyone was casing the area before that."

Jake's fingers fly over the keyboard, and within moments, he has the six screens in front of him showing various angles of my apartment. We see nothing of interest on the first day, but on the second, we see Sophie enter the hallway to my floor, then open the door and go inside. An hour later, she's back on the camera carrying trash to the disposal shoot on the next hallway, and that's when we see Langdon skulking in from the other side and entering my place. Obviously, his mother hadn't locked the door behind her because he doesn't pause long. Jake snorts in amusement, seeming almost proud of his new charge. Nic jots down a couple of tag numbers from vehicles we spot more than once, but I figure most live in the area. I'm returning a text to my father when Nic punches me in the arm hard enough to push my chair to the side a few inches. *What the...?*

"You fucked the dry cleaner's daughter?" he asks incredulously. "I've asked her out a dozen times and gotten nowhere. Hell, she doesn't even speak English." She does speak English, but that's beside the point here. *Fuck, how I wish I could turn back time.* I have no clue why, since discussing past conquests is nothing new—but I feel like a pig. No, wait. Hadn't Nina referred to me as a junkyard dog in one of her notes? Made me long for the more formal Mr. Moretti greeting she mostly used. Granted, I generally refrain from broadcasting my intimate encounters all over the office. *Fuck, there hadn't been any to broadcast recently, until that lapse in judgment.* But it's not unusual for Nic to comment on someone I've been with.

"Her grasp of our language isn't the best," I acknowledge. "And she asked me out for a drink."

"According to the kid, there's nothing wrong with her pipes." Jake smirks. "Apparently, she can damn near shatter glass with the right... incentive."

"I'd hate you if I didn't admire you so much," Nic deadpans. "Wait"—he raps his knuckles on the table loudly— "she was the blonde Langdon heard?" Jake shoots Nic a look of disbelief. It fucks with me, though, because firstly, he knows me well enough to not be questioning my skills, but secondly... *Nina.* I like to fuck. I'm a man. So be it. But I somehow feel dirty that *she* now knows, and I'm not entirely sure why.

I'm so distracted by their bickering that I almost miss the figure on one of the monitors. "Hey, back that frame up," I snap, pointing at the image in question. Jake immediately stops speaking midsentence and turns to see what has my attention. Nic and I get to our feet and move closer as he hits the play button once again. A figure slides out feet first from one of my apartment windows. When they make contact with the small platform connected to the fire escape, they stand, holding on to the railing while looking down at something. They're clothed from head to foot in black and are small in stature. "Can you zoom in closer?

If they look up, we might get a better view." Jake makes the necessary adjustments, and we all wait with bated breath, hoping for anything that gives us a clue who the intruder is. They're moving down the stairs now, and their head is almost out of sight when they pause for a moment and look up. Jake freezes the shot without being told, and I stare in disbelief.

It can't be.

What the fuck?

"I'm just going to go ahead and put it out there," Nic mutters dryly, "but that sure resembles a certain houseguest you have. Might not be the world's clearest picture, but toss in the size and the face, and that's enough to make you ask questions."

"She wouldn't," I croak. "There's a big drop at the end of those stairs. She's gonna break her fucking neck."

Jake appears to be running through the footage from another angle, and a few minutes later, he points at the second screen. "Unbelievable," he says dazedly. I can't believe my eyes when she swings from the bottom rung and grabs the drainage pipe. Then she shimmies down the remainder of the way and leaps neatly to her feet before disappearing down the alley and out of sight.

"At the risk of being stabbed," Nic interjects, "I'm strangely turned on right now."

"That makes two of us." Jake waves a hand, before dropping it quickly when he sees my frown.

"Check the rest of the footage and see when she comes back." I'm blown away that she was not only that brazen but also that damn stupid. Has she completely forgotten the reason she's staying with me? Did running around alone in the middle of the night not set off any kind of alarm bells for her?

Ten minutes later, Jake drops into a chair, and the rest of us follow suit. "I would have never believed it," he says. "She's done the same thing every night since then. And it's mostly the same scenario. Gone a couple of hours, then she crawls up the drain and leaps over to the fire escape stairs."

"She's going to give me some fucking answers," I hiss as anger churns through my veins. She could have broken her fool neck, and I wouldn't have known it for hours. *Where the fuck is she going?*

I have my hand on the doorknob when Nic stops me. "If you show your hand now, you might never get the truth. I know you're pissed, but if you go charging in and attack her, she'll lockdown. Keep your shit together and follow her little Houdini ass tonight. Let's see what she's up to. None of us want to believe it, but she could be in this mess up to her pretty neck. As angry as she is at you, she damn sure isn't going to confess to anything, *Mr. Moretti.*"

"As much as it pains me to admit it, he's got a point," Jake agrees ruefully. "I'll go back and watch all the footage again to make sure we didn't miss anything else. But it's doubtful she met anyone close enough to the building for us to have picked them up on camera."

It's not typically something I do, but I say, "Let's keep what we've seen in this room to ourselves for now. She's in enough danger without us bringing more attention down on her. There are those who don't like or agree with our decision to offer her sanctuary because she's a Gavino. This could be a smoking gun for the wrong person."

"Agreed," Nic says without hesitation. He might not get along with Minka, but he has a soft spot for Nina. *Why does that bother me so much?* "Don't get me wrong, I don't buy it for a minute that she's anything other than her usual—in the wrong place at the wrong time. But she can't expect us to put our asses on the line to cover hers if she's hiding shit. I knew the moment she held a gun on my dick that she was no timid spinster. But, gotta say, climbing up and down the side of your building is more than I would have given her credit for. Did you notice that there was no hesitation at all? She's agile as a fucking cat. That wasn't her first time doing it." He shakes his head before adding, "Bet she gave old Franklin a stomach ulcer, the little hellion."

"And she seems so sweet on the surface," Jake muses. "Like a pretty china doll with a banging—" He stops abruptly when Nic makes a chopping gesture.

"Why is it all right for you to say stuff like that about her and not him?" I ask in exasperation.

Nic appears to give it serious thought for all of five seconds. "Well,

I'm older by a few years, so there's seniority, plus you know I'm merely kidding. I'd never try to poach your goods." His attempt to reassure me just pisses Jake off. I swear, he doesn't connect all the dots before he opens his mouth. "I didn't mean it like that," he says. "You know what, let's just sideline this particular topic. Our time would be better spent putting a plan together for tonight. I'll even take first watch if you two will stop your fucking whining. Swear to God, when did everyone become such sensitive bitches?"

Grinning despite myself, I do as he's suggested because he's right for once. This isn't the time for high school drama. I've trusted these men with my life more times than I can count. Their loyalty to me is unquestionable. I damn sure have no reason to be jealous or suspicious. *Yeah, because the woman in question hates you. Doesn't belong to you—never will.* I motion for them to join me at the table once more. "All right, let's tail her tonight. Jake, reposition the cameras to scan as much of the surrounding areas as possible. Hell, install another in the alley if necessary to cover it fully. The timestamp on her excursions shows her leaving just after midnight and returning around two. I'll make up some excuse and meet you both in the lobby at twenty-two hundred. Jake will keep eyes on the fire escape." I motion to Nic as I say, "We'll spread out a mile in every direction to see if anything looks out of place."

Jake remains behind to continue reviewing the footage while Nic and I walk down the long hallway that always feels a bit like a crypt to me. *Probably not the best of comparisons right now.* "Is it just me or is everything falling apart around us? I know we've been in a lot of tough spots before, but there's just a different feeling in the air. Know what I mean?"

You have no fucking clue brother—not an inkling. "Yeah." I nod, then search for words of reassurance that are slow coming. "Guess it's the fact that there's so much coming at us with damn little time to recover in between. Remember when Anthony had all that shit going on with his uncle? Shit will mess with your head after a while."

"It's a mindfuck all right," he replies. "It has me suspicious of my own blood and the guys I grew up with. Some are assholes or morons, but I trust them because I never had a reason not to. Now I look at them twice, wondering if we have a traitor in our own fucking house." He continues speaking while I fight the urge to puke. Logically I'm aware he hasn't a clue what's really going on behind the scenes, but still, he's thrusting a knife in my gut and turning the handle with every word he utters. "I mean, I don't know Langdon personally, and the Gavino casualties are tough, but it's the nature of the beast. That attempt on you, though, I still can't get that out of my mind. It was so fucking close to taking both you and Nina out."

We're standing in the middle of the courtyard now. Men are moving around in the distance, but none of them appears to have any interest in our presence. "You said it yourself, Nic, it is the reality in our world. Doesn't make it suck any less, but it's far from the first or last time there'll be unrest among the families—or even within our own."

"I feel you"—he shakes his head— "but what it's really brought home to me is how lax we've become with our lives. Hell, last year when you were poisoned, that should have been a wake-up call. And yeah, we doubled down and added extra security where we were vulnerable, but we've gradually relaxed, and someone slipped through the cracks in our foundation. Which one of us must die for us to finally accept that we're not invincible? Unless there's something I don't know, none of us has been blessed with immortality. A bullet to the head will drop the toughest motherfucker out there. Goddamn, even Nina has been sneaking out of your place for a week and going who knows where before letting herself back in. She's a chick with no real mafia survival training, yet she bypassed our guys easily. Hell, she was probably standing in front of them waving her hands and sticking her tongue out. A fat lot of good it would have done. We survived for a long time on our reputation and that of Draco's. We show enough brute strength at the right times to keep the wrong people at bay, but they're getting braver and a fuck of a lot more brazen. We have got to make sure our house is in order and that the Morettis are protected on all fronts."

It's probably the most serious and impassioned speech I've ever heard Nic deliver. If he's this worried, then we're on a whole new playing field. That's the bad thing about fear and unease; it spreads like the fucking plague. Overthinking can kill just as surely as *under*thinking. I don't disagree with what he's said. How could I? It's true. And changes must be made. But while we're doing that, it's imperative we project confidence to our men and our enemies. The Morettis don't run, nor do they fear anyone. "You're not wrong, brother. But it must be handled with discretion. I can't believe I'm saying this, but you need to remain the cocky fucker you've always been when others are around. We'll meet with my father soon, but in the meantime, keep it casual. Fight smarter and not harder, right?" I bump my shoulder into his. "Turn that frown upside down, cupcake."

He chokes on the endearment, but his smile is back in place. "I know you're having problems with your woman, but I don't fly that way, dude. You got a hankering to bat for the same team, you should hit up Jake first. I've always wondered about him. I swear his last girlfriend looked just like our uncle Albert. You ever notice that? When she smiled, there was that same freaky dent in her face."

"Pretty sure those are called dimples," I point out diplomatically, but it's hard not to agree. She had been a touch masculine. She thumped me on the back once and damn near sent me sprawling.

He raises his brows skeptically. "You can call them what you want, but you know where I'm coming from. Personally, I think he was afraid to dump her ass. Figured she'd kill him. Was a smart move to let her break it off. But man, that had to be humiliating being dumped by a chick that goddamn ugly. That's a big blow to your pride. No wonder he hasn't gotten back out there yet."

At some point, we begin walking again, and we're standing next to our vehicles when he finishes outlining Jake's love life. "I'd keep that insight to myself if I were you," I advise wryly. I open my door, then turn back to say, "Meet me in the garage tonight. I'd rather Nina not see you hanging around. It might spook her into calling her midnight stroll off. Oh... how are things going with Minka?" It hadn't occurred to me before, but it's kind of strange that he hasn't said a single word about her. Fuck, I hope he hasn't lost his shit and killed her. *That would likely be the other way around.*

He shrugs nonchalantly. "Same ole shit, different day. Kind of like a badass rash that never heals."

"That's a step up for you two." I smirk. "That's damn near a declaration of love. She's hot in a serial killer kind of way. Keep your distance, though. She'd probably make Jake's ex seem tame in comparison."

"You got that right." He grins but doesn't add anything more. Normally, this would have him off on another tangent, but he doesn't go there. It's possible he's still dwelling on our earlier conversation. Hopefully, I can put his mind at ease tonight.

We get into our matching black Escalades, and I pull out ahead of him. I drive slowly to intentionally delay my arrival home. This shit with Nina has shaken me more than I let on to Nic and Jake. In a weird way, I feel almost betrayed, which makes zero sense because she's basically a stranger to me. Yeah, I've known her for a while now, but I can't even call us friends. She could be fucking Wonder Woman, and I'd be none the wiser. Hell, maybe she is. She certainly navigated her way down from four floors up without so much as a pause. I couldn't name another female off the top of my head who'd attempt that. Plenty of men would balk as well.

The thought has crossed my mind that she might be involved with someone. She was smart enough not to invite them over to my place, so sneaking around would make sense. *What kind of pussy would let his woman put herself in danger for a hookup?* Might not even be about sex but seemed a bit like a booty call. When I find out who he is, I won't kill him. I'll just make him wish he were dead. *Things that psychos say for two hundred, Alex.* Maybe I should lay off watching *Jeopardy.* Swear to fuck, she's driving me insane. She's been living with me for all of a week, and I've turned into a jealous fool. Which is sheer torture. She won't speak to me, but my entire place smells like her. That makes it so much worse. I can't escape her, and I'm surrounded. Just imagining another man having similar thoughts is enough to send my blood pressure skyrocketing. *Mine.* I'm beginning to think I should stay at the apartment and have Jake take my place. I'm honestly afraid I'll lose it if I find her with someone else. I have no claim at all, yet in my mind, she's belonged to me since that day she found me in the woods. I'd been convinced I was dying, and opening my eyes to see that beautiful angel filled me with a strange kind of peace. If her face was the last thing I saw before I checked out of this world, then I couldn't ask for much more than that. Of course, seconds later, I puked all over both of us, thus effectively ruining the moment. Months have passed since then, but my desire for her has only gotten stronger. Yeah, I'm obsessed with fucking her, but that's not all. I want to possess every part of her. For Nina, I'd do the dog and pony show. Flowers, some mushy stuff, whatever made her look at me as a man and not a mafia thug. *And there's why you feel like a bastard for fucking Rayna last week.* Nina was right to hate me, and *I doubt that will ever change now, asshole.*

I pull into the parking garage and cut the engine. I can no longer put it off. This is one time it'll be a plus to be ignored. If I can avoid interacting with her now, it'll make keeping it together easier. Because if she provokes me, I fear all reason will flee, and I'll ruin our chances of finding out where she's going every night. I wonder if that's not really what I want. Jack Nicholson said it best in *A Few Good Men*. "You can't handle the truth." It might have been a different scenario, but it damn well rings true for me.

I slip the key in the deadbolt and unlock the door, before pushing it open. It takes about five seconds to know I'm fucked. I may not be the best at reading women, but when one greets you with a smile after ignoring your very existence for days, you're in trouble. If I had any sense at all, I'd run, but instead, I close the door behind me and wonder why I feel as if I'm going to war.

Nina

I bite my tongue to keep from grinning as Marco shifts uneasily. It hasn't been easy, but I'm proud of the fact that I've maintained my silence. I planned to be bitchy and snide after he cut me off so rudely that night, but Minka suggested a different approach, and I'll admit, it's been successful. He hasn't caved and called me out on it, but it's obviously bothered him—a lot. My mom often did the same thing to Franklin when she was angry, but I've never been one to play games. To me, if that was necessary, then the relationship was over before it ever started. *What relationship?* I silence that pesky voice in my head with the rationalization even friendships fall under that category. There is some unique factor that exists between you and the people in your life. And if any of them requires deceit, then you're better off without them. *What do you call sneaking out every night?* That wouldn't be necessary if I wasn't under lock and key here. *You do still have your phone. Ever heard of texting or calling?* Damn, I hate the stuff that goes through my mind. What makes me a good writer also makes me a big over analyzer. I can argue ten different points with myself for hours. All sides have an opinion, and none of them ever agree. I realize I've been quiet for too long. I wanted to unnerve him, not have him perform CPR on me. *On second thought...* "How was your day? Things go well at—work?" *Kill or torture anyone, dear?* I have to commend myself on delivering that last question with a straight face.

He blinks, then does it again before saying slowly, "It was fine. Nothing out of the normal. You?"

"Oh, just great here. I hope you don't mind, but I had one of your men pick up a few things for me at the supermarket."

His face reddens. God, he is blushing, and it's so hot. He looks down at his feet as he murmurs, "Um, yeah, no problem. I know you needed... some girl things."

I draw a complete blank. *What's he talking about?* He probably has me confused with one of his *women.* I open my mouth, ready to deliver a scathing comment when it hits me. *The note.* That was one of my finer moments in my campaign to torture him. I laughed so hard when I wrote it. There aren't many men out there who want to shop for or talk about your period. It had been a toss-up between that and diarrhea. I figured either would freak him out. Plus picturing him in a store shopping for tampons was too good to resist. *Wait—speaking of.* I almost let it go, but wouldn't that throw my credibility in question? I frown, attempting to appear concerned. "I—I thought you were bringing those home. I didn't ask Matt for... that. I would have been too embarrassed." I wring my hands together, the picture of anxiety. *I might be overplaying this a bit.* "I used my last tampon today. It's going to be a long night." He flinches when I ask, "Do you have a mattress protector? Oh, and maybe extra toilet paper?" He stands rooted in place for a full minute. I'm tempted to poke him to see if he's in some kind of trance. Then he spins on his heel and leaves the apartment.

"Didn't see that one coming," I mutter under my breath. I'm convinced he's in his car speeding toward Walgreens when he returns.

"It's being taken care of," he says by way of explanation. "You hungry? Take your pick from the menus and let me know what you're in the mood for."

I recall the surprise I planned to spring on him before the whole tampon distraction. "No need. I cooked. That's what I had Matt pick up. You do like lasagna, right? I love Italian food."

Clearly taken aback, he nods, then appears to relax. *Stop being so damn sexy, Moretti, because you're making me feel guilty.* "It's my favorite. My mom makes sauce that cooks damn near all day. I told her once to buy it in a jar like everyone else." He rubs the back of his head before shooting me a grin that singes my panties. *Wooza.* "She smacked me with a wooden spoon and told me to never speak of such in her kitchen again."

"I'd like to meet your mother." I laugh at his pained expression. "I think we'd get along well. She can show me all your baby pictures. Were you chubby? Take a bath with a rubber ducky? Wait, I bet you were a bed wetter, right?" Who knew the man had so many triggers? I've stumbled on half a dozen in the past ten minutes alone. *And why did they make me like him more?* Even when he was throwing up in my apartment after being poisoned, there was something special about him—almost otherworldly. But when he's talking about his mother, he seems human. Like any other man who both adores and fears the woman who gave him life. It's a sweet side of him that I find tugs at my heart. I'm so tempted to abort the horrible dinner that awaits him, but he deserves it. This is my final retaliation for the blow he dealt to my pride—and my feelings—a week ago, and I need to see it through. *What man can kiss a woman with such need and passion and then toss her away moments later as irrelevant?* A man whose life will never include an outsider.

Instead of looking offended, he simply laughs at the suggestions I've thrown out. "Who the hell knows? It was a long time ago. I'm sure my mom would be thrilled to give you the lowdown on every embarrassing moment in my life in both written and verbal form. Probably has graphs and spreadsheets along with a PowerPoint presentation." He winces and points at the kitchen. "Before my appetite is ruined, let's eat. I have a couple of bottles of wine that will go well with lasagna. Sound good?"

I nod, thinking he'll need more than Merlot to make his dinner palatable. I have everything set up on the bar in the kitchen, and I spoon out a heaping portion of lasagna for him. I've also mixed up a salad with some homemade dressing that consists of garlic flakes, basil, a ton of salt, and oil. Luckily, his back is turned, so he doesn't see that my food is already on my plate. *Stouffer's makes kickass Italian.* I take my seat just in time to see him bend over to pick up the napkin he dropped in the floor. *Can I have the envelope, please? Award for the world's greatest ass goes to . . .* "Marco." *Oh shit.* My silent ogling just became verbal.

He turns, raising a brow. "What's that, Belle?"

He has no clue how much I secretly love that nickname. I'm not deluded; I know I'm not special to him, but I can't help but feel that way when he calls me that in a tone that almost sounds affectionate. *The blonde screamer probably harbors the same kind of pathetic hope.* Thoughts of the woman I've never met but heard far too much about effectively douse any lingering guilt over this meal from hell I've prepared. "Oh, nothing." I wave my hand casually. "The wine looks good." *The wine looks good? It looks the same as every other Merlot in the world, idiot.*

He shows no indication that he found my comment bizarre. A testament to how much he's gotten used to the crazy stuff I say. He puts my glass in front of me, then takes his seat. I swallow the lump in my throat as he loads his fork with a bite big enough to choke a horse. His face goes from relaxed, to puzzled, to dismayed. I wait, expecting him to grab a napkin and spit it out, but he doesn't. Instead, he swallows audibly, then washes it down with half a glass of wine. I must admit, I'm impressed. I expected at least some profanity, but he hasn't uttered a word. Yet. His eyes dart to the salad, and I can almost hear his inner voice telling him that it must be a safer choice. Seconds later, he discovers it's far from that. The whole thing was meant as a payback. I should be overcome with mirth—doing everything I can to hold the laughter inside—yet something strange is happening instead. As he goes in for another—much smaller bite of lasagna—I feel a bit like the Grinch. For surely my heart has grown three sizes or more watching him eat a meal that isn't fit for human consumption. And I have a sneaking suspicion he's enduring the punishment to avoid offending me. As if I need another reason to be captivated by this man. I set out to prove a point tonight, and instead, he's served up a truth to me.

He's a gentleman.

Not one scathing comment. Not one snide remark to tease or aggravate me. *After a week of my silence and churlish behavior. If I'm truly honest,* he doesn't owe me anything. Why did I think we were suddenly a team anyway? Was I upset for Langdon? Yes, my God, yes. The kid lost his whole family, and I know exactly what that's like. But I'm not here as a team member. I'm simply being kept safe. And somehow, not only has he stolen my thirst for revenge, but I fear he's also taken my anger with it. It makes sense why I'm attracted to Marco Moretti. Yes, he's a stunning man, but I can now see even more of his good traits to know he isn't like any other man I know, and that's what worries me the most. *Will my heart survive this?*

6

Marco

Fuck me running, this is the worst meal of my life. *Then why did you ask for seconds?* And the salad—how could you possibly screw up a leaf of lettuce? I had to wonder if it was just me because she appears to be enjoying her food. Licked her fork before setting it down. She's eaten as much or more than I have. If this is an example of her cooking, she probably killed her taste buds years ago. That must be it. Damn things have packed up and got the hell out. "The lasagna has an . . . interesting texture. I assume the green stuff is spinach, but how about this?" I hold my fork closer for inspection, and she peers down before nodding.

Her eyes shift for a moment, and she looks almost guilty at my words. I'm afraid I've hurt her feelings, but she bounces back quickly. "I can't be sure since it's covered in sauce, but it's probably one of the anchovies. Don't you think they really give it something extra? I love to experiment with recipes and make them my own. Everyone always said I was nuts for adding grape jelly to my marinara too, but you can't argue with the results, can you?"

My stomach lurches precariously, and I'm afraid I'm going to blow right here. Fucking hell, the petite beauty grinning so sweetly across the bar at me can't cook for shit. No, scratch that, I'd rather she serves me straight-up shit. At least then I'd know what I was eating. But now, it's like a surprise pack of random ingredients that adds up to the worst thing I've ever tasted. I'm afraid to ask her about the salad. She probably mixed Drano with canola oil. *Don't think about it. Block it out. Take one for the team. Suffer in silence. Don't shit your pants.* Of all the mental suggestions flying my way, the last one is most important. Hell, knowing my luck, there's not a single square of toilet paper in the whole place. *I've thought about shit entirely too much since we met.*

I take another gulp of wine and almost panic when I see my glass is empty. That's it. Dinner is officially over. No way can I ingest more without a substantial amount of alcohol to lessen the pain. *Fuck, the slimy noodles.* Actually, those had been a plus. There was no need to chew as they simply slid right down. "Most memorable dinner ever," I say weakly. "I... I'll clean up now since you cooked." *Or so I thought.* It was more like an hour later when I could safely leave the bathroom. She's put everything away, hopefully in a biohazard box. I swear, if I so much as spot a container of leftovers in the refrigerator, I'll burn down my apartment and have the land beneath it declared a toxic dump.

She's wringing her damn hands again and pacing the living room when I return. She spots me and rushes over, laying a hand on my arm. "Are you all right? You ran out of the kitchen so fast I didn't know what to think. I stood outside the bathroom door for a few minutes in case you needed help."

Fuck me. The look on her face tells me everything I never wanted to know—ever. I've heard women, including my mother, complain about men being babies when they're sick. That might be the case in some instances, but after you've blown out the plumbing with a hot chick just feet away, yeah, not so much. You don't want to be cuddled or waited on. You simply wish to pretend it never happened and hope to fuck she'll go along with it. So far, Nina hasn't gotten the silent memo. "I'm good," I say easily, then attempt a subject change. "It's about time for your favorite television show again, isn't it? Bet you can't wait to find out what happened to old Mick." *And yes, I know his name is Rick, but I get off on teasing her.*

True to form, Nina is like a dog with a bone. She completely disregards my topic shift and goes right back to ground zero. "I looked through your cabinets, but you don't have anything for your stomach. I hope it's okay that I asked one of your men to run to the store for some Pepto-Bismol." I'd think she's fucking with me if she didn't look so concerned when she adds, "I thought about asking for Imodium as well, but that's not a good idea if you have a stomach bug. Wait, maybe we should text him and have him pick some up anyway. Better safe than sorry."

Oh, I'm sorry all right—so fucking sorry that I'll be the joke of every Moretti within an hour. I've barely finished that thought when my doorbell rings. *Goddammit.* She looks over at me, and I at her, but neither of us moves. Then a knock sounds along with a loud voice bellowing out, "Hey boss, everything cool in there? I got your stuff the little lady asked for." *Not Wade. Anyone but him. He gossips like a fucking girl.*

Nina points toward the door before asking, "Should I get that?"

I release a sigh that's loud enough to be heard on the other end of town. Then I stalk across the room and unlock the deadbolt. When I see a grinning Wade standing there, I want to bury my fist in his face so damn bad that my fingers twitch. He's never been particularly smart; otherwise, he'd toss the huge bag he's holding at me and run for his life. But no, he doesn't move a muscle. Instead, he holds it up for my inspection. "Got everything on the list, plus a little extra." He's notorious for having a juvenile sense of humor, so I fully expect him to pull out a gas mask or something along those lines. Turns out, that's just wishful thinking on my part. Instead, he begins rummaging through the bag before handing me the first box.

"Stefan suggested gas drops since the little lady mentioned you were holding your stomach. Those things really help take the edge off, if you get my drift." *The fucker is dead. Wherever Jimmy Hoffa went, Wade Moretti will be joining him very soon.* Could he possibly be this stupid? There isn't a man alive who wouldn't flee from the look on my face right now, but he appears clueless. A moment later, he comes up with some sort of tube. "Big Joey recommended this here butt cream. Says the wife puts it on Little Joey's ass when he's got the runs. Supposed to be some good shit. Whoops, bad choice of words there."

"Get the fuck out," I hiss between clenched teeth. "If I see you again this year, I'll let Nic shoot you and your fucking dog." *All right, that last part is a lie. I like the dog better than him.*

Yet he doesn't move or appear alarmed by my threats. What little patience I had is gone, and my hand is scant inches from his face when he thrusts a package against my chest. "From Nic," he tosses out quickly. *Hadn't seen that coming.* Best of all, he leaves before I'm forced to dirty up the hallway with blood. Plus, Nina would likely stop speaking to me again. Leave me one of her crazy notes addressed to *Mr. Moretti. Maybe I should write her a fucking note about her cooking skills. Offer her a million bucks to never even think about lasagna again, much less make it.* My stomach makes a growling noise as if agreeing wholeheartedly.

I'm tempted to leave everything, but I know Nina will insist on getting it. So I shift the things in my arms to one side and lean down to pick up the bag from the floor. I kick the door shut with my foot and nearly plow into her. At some point, she moved from the living room to the entryway. No doubt she heard Wade's entire comedy routine. *I should have shot him.* "Wow, that looks like more than Pepto-Bismol." She takes a step closer and tilts her head. Then her mouth twitches. "Do you require those often?" she asks as she pulls the first package from under my arm.

The motherfucker. I was so frustrated with the imbecile that I didn't bother to look at what he gave me last. Just what I always wanted—an economy-sized bag of adult diapers. *How long was I in the bathroom?* I know Wade has a big mouth, but this is impressive even for him. He was either lying, or he managed to tell half the family about my unfortunate stomach problems. While Nina laughs and clutches the pack of Depends to her chest like her favorite stuffed animal, I absently pull my phone from my pocket when it chimes and see a text from Nic.

NIC: We still on for tonight or are you holding court?

Does everyone speak in riddles now? Even though it makes no sense, which is usually the case with Nic, at least it's not another toilet joke.

ME: What the fuck?

I take the other bag to the kitchen and place it on the bar. Thankfully, Nina doesn't follow. She's probably too busy snapping a picture of the diapers and uploading it to every social media site she can think of. *#Marcoshithispants.* Even I must admit, that thought is kind of funny.

NIC: You know, since you're riding your throne. Sounded as if it might be a long-term kind of problem.

So much for being amused. I should have known it was too much to hope for that I wasn't the ass of everyone's jokes tonight.

ME: Shut the fuck up and be here as planned.

I'm tempted to throw my phone on the floor and stomp on it a few times, but find the strength to resist. I glance at my watch and see that I have a few hours until I meet him. *Just in case.* I grab a bottle of water from the refrigerator and toss back a couple of gas drops, then chew a Pepto tablet for added insurance. There is no way in hell I'll ever live it down if I have a relapse while I'm with Nic tonight. I'll wear one of the diapers before I let that happen.

I nearly squeal like a girl when Nina suddenly says, "I'm sorry about all that. I should have thought it through first." It's getting downright humiliating the way she catches me unaware so much. If she were the bad guy, I'd have been dead many times over by now. *If that meal doesn't make her the enemy, I don't know what does.*

I take my time replacing the cap on the bottle and setting it aside before slowly turning to face her. I see remorse in her eyes, but the slight curve of those plump lips also shows a hint of amusement. I can't even fault her for it. Not many could have made it through Wade's performance without falling victim to his annoying humor. I shrug my shoulders indifferently. "In case you didn't know, men love nothing better than heckling each other. The cruder, the better. Not to worry, by tomorrow they'll have moved on to someone else." *Not likely, at least without the threat of death and dismemberment.*

She leans against the cabinet behind her and rolls her eyes. "It's a bit juvenile, isn't it? Making fun of another's misfortune. It happens to everyone at some point."

"If it had been Wade or Nic, hell, any of them, I'd have joined in. So don't be outraged on my behalf. I assure you I give as good, no, usually better than I get. We all pay the price occasionally, Belle. It's not personal; it's a guy thing."

Instead of laughing, she appears faintly disgusted now. It's never wise to overshare with a woman. They grow out of such childish antics early in life. Men only get more creative and nastier. "No wonder I've had so many dates from hell. And here I thought it was simply bad luck. I'd be better off as a lesbian." *Sweet Lord, roll your tongue back in.* Fuck yeah, it's true, there is nothing hotter than two chicks going at it. It's yet another guy thing. Pretty sure I should keep that to myself though. She places a finger on her chin as if seriously considering the matter. "I wonder if Minka would be interested in taking our relationship to the next level? We already love and respect each other. We've seen each other naked more times than I can count." *Fuck, say that again and lick your lips.* "We have no secrets, so that's a big one out of the way." *Speaking of big ones.* I discreetly readjust as she continues her list. "All men are pigs and neither of us have gotten lucky in a million years. Plus, you can pick up a vibrator at convenience stores now, so what do you need a man for?"

She pauses as if waiting. *She seriously wants me to answer that?* "Er— to take the trash out? Buy you dinner, piss you off, and break your heart?" *Again, too much sharing of information.*

"You forgot the part about leaving you hanging after getting themselves off. There are so many self-help books for women it makes me wonder why no one has written one for men. Quite obviously, it's urgently needed. You're either clueless or just too lazy to care that a woman doesn't come."

Whoa. Say what? Suddenly, this seems so much more personal. Hell, I'm offended, and we've never had sex, so I'm not the dude who didn't bring it home. *So why do I feel guilty?* I lazily close the distance between us. Going off half-cocked will only make her bolt. My hands don't leave my side when I reach her. Instead, my body just grazes hers. I keep my face impassive even as I hear her draw a ragged breath. She's wearing a long gray top and some black pants underneath that look like a second skin. *Bad wardrobe choice, sweetheart.* The thin material does nothing to hide the clear outline of her nipples. Granted, she could be cold; in fact, I believe I feel her shivering. I lean closer and lower my face to within an inch of her neck. I inhale, intoxicated by her scent. Then I exhale harder than necessary so she'll feel my breath against her sensitive skin. My tongue darts out, and I take a long, leisurely lick of the pulse beating frantically there. She cries out and shifts closer, but I refuse to be hurried.

My lips are only inches from her earlobe when I whisper, "Belle, the only way I'll come is if you've already gotten yours many times." She's lost in the moment, moving restlessly against me, wanting what I've promised. I'm not even sure she's aware of what she's silently asking for —but I am. And unfortunately, I can't give it to either of us now because it would be rushed, and I refuse to let that happen. Especially considering what she's revealed. A quick orgasm isn't going to make up for a lifetime of neglect. We may have no future together, but she will have a night that she'll never forget. This is no longer about proving a point. It's about giving an amazing woman an experience she's never had and deserves. Hell, every woman deserves to be put first in bed. Even rushed, I'd never get off and walk away, so she has every right to be bitter. If you don't please your woman, you're not a man. I've been with some crazy chicks in my time, but at the end of the day, I love everything about the opposite sex. We should be on our knees thanking them—no, worshipping them—for even giving us a second glance, much less sleeping with us. My mouth settles against hers, but instead of slipping my tongue into her mouth, I nip her bottom lip with my teeth gently, and she hisses in response. *Fuck.* I want to deepen the kiss so fucking much that I can barely stop myself. But I can't risk it. She's my weakness. I've known it since we met. So I toss aside my pride and grab the only lifeline available. With a herculean effort, I push away and call out as I flee, "Sorry, Belle, not feeling well again."

It's not exactly a lie. Leaving her looking like every wet dream I've ever had is making me ache all over. I've never had sexual frustration so bad that my teeth hurt, but they do now. *Maybe I'm getting the flu.* Making it to the main bathroom and shutting the door is the equivalent of crossing the finish line in a cross-country race. I'm in the process of splashing cold water on my face when I come to the realization that drastic measures are needed. I'm going to jack off instead of fucking a willing woman. I'm fucking obsessed with her, and if this wasn't so pitiful, I would laugh.

Instead, I turn the water in the sink up to full blast to provide some sound coverage, flip on the fan since she already thinks I'm having another emergency, and lower my zipper. I don't bother attempting to prolong the moment since this is about a straight-up release. I'm already turned on, so no foreplay is needed. It only takes an embarrassingly few rough jerks, and I'm blowing my load into a hand towel. I feel lightheaded for a moment and lean against the wall, closing my eyes until it's passed. Then I clean up and smile wryly despite myself. In all the time I've lived in this apartment, I don't think I've ever spent this much time in the bathroom.

I'm tempted to stay a little longer, but I'm afraid the uncertainty will derail her usual evening plans. Come to think of it, I see no reason not to use my stomach issues as an excuse to turn in early. That's a bonus in more than one way. I can avoid fucking her on the sofa, countertop, against the wall... *Focus, that's not helping. Think of Nic laughing at you.* The last thought works like a charm, and it's back to the business. I don't risk telling her face to face. Instead, I call out the lie from the hallway and escape to the guest room. I text Nic and delay our meeting for another half hour to give her plenty of time to feel confident I'm asleep.

I'm apprehensive about what I'll discover tonight. I have no room to judge her if she's deceiving me because I've been doing that very thing to her all along. But fuck, I want to believe that she's better than that—

better than me. To find out otherwise would kill the only part of me that's not completely jaded. One way or the other, whatever this is between us will change tonight. And I'm not sure I'm ready for that. She'll either remain on a pedestal, or she'll be in hell next to me. The only thing certain is that I want her either way—that's never in question. Nor is the sad fact that she'll end up hating me... along with everyone else.

Nina

It's been an hour since Marco disappeared into his room. I've been to the door three times in the past fifteen minutes but haven't detected any signs of life. After all he's been through tonight, he has to be asleep —right? It's almost time to leave, and even though I've changed into more comfortable clothing, I'm still filled with indecision. What if there's an emergency, and he needs me before I get back? I always lock my door from the inside, so if it's urgent enough for him to wake me, he probably won't have the strength to break in. He'll do what any normal person would and call 9-1-1. Or in his case, he'll summons one of the men who are always close by. Heck, he practically bolted from the kitchen earlier and hasn't come back to say good night in person. *Would you after that?* He's more likely to stab me in my sleep than ask me for help.

Even though I try to assuage my guilt by saying he deserved the near poisoning I gave him via lasagna, I still feel bad. I expected to have some laughs at his expense. Especially, when I told him the truth later, and he realized I'd paid him back. But there's no way in hell I'll admit it now. Not after how sick he's been. Minka and I laughed on the phone as I threw every random thing I could find in my pasta creation from hell. It was supposed to be funny. Actually, Minka found it hilarious—even more so with the stomach problems it caused. She dedicated a solid five minutes to bathroom humor, and I tried not to laugh. But it had been impossible a few times.

I feel my pocket vibrate and glance around before pulling out my phone.

I'll see you soon. On my way.

I know this is a mistake. I can feel it in my very bones. But even as I berate myself for being a fool, I carefully press my ear against his door one last time. Hearing nothing, I go into my room and gently ease the door shut. The lock sounds like a gunshot in the silence, but I know it's simply nerves amplifying everything.

I've perfected sneaking out for my nightly excursion. The first time, I was hesitant and more than a little afraid of either falling or getting caught. Like every rebellious teenager, I've scaled plenty of walls and drainpipes in my adolescence. And a few times since in an emergency. Even though it has been a while, I surprised myself by having no problems at all. Once you've done something like that successfully, you feel almost invincible.

The biggest challenge was the window sensors. Luckily, on the first day here, Jake took the alarm system offline to make some changes to it. And Marco nicely left a paper with the new code on the coffee table. After he pissed me off, I put my time that night to good use. While he was on his phone, I located the panel in the entryway and keyed in the new code. My hands shook so badly I was sure I'd hit the wrong sequence and end up sleeping with the fishes. But thanks to the fact that it was the same model as Franklin's, I navigated it easily. In less than two minutes, I deactivated the window sensors for Marco's bedroom and exited the programming. Then I tiptoed back to his room and used a nail file from my purse to unscrew the sensor pads and remove them. Thankfully, he hasn't insisted on having his room back, or it would have all been for nothing. I haven't spent half my life around the Gavinos without learning a thing or two, and there aren't too many places I can't break in to or out of. Of course, Minka is far better at it than I am. She broke into a bank at the age of fourteen on a dare. She said her father had been so pissed off at her—but had bragged about it to others for years.

I'm almost on autopilot as I leap from the fire escape to the drainage gutter. I learned after the first night that wearing gloves was a necessity. They allowed me to slide instead of a weird, backward crawl. I crouch when my feet hit the ground. After scanning the area, I ease into the shadows and take off at a run. Three blocks later, I duck into a parking garage and go to the last spot. I absently pat my hair to make sure it's still secured in a tight bun before tossing my leg over the sports bike and pulling the key from my pocket.

Yet another thing I had to thank Minka for. That my best friend had always been a tomboy certainly served us well through the years, and remaining in her shadow most of our life worked in my favor. No one paid me much attention because she was the hellion. I was the good girl she led astray on occasion. They had no clue I was often just as guilty, if not more so, than she was. It was our version of good cop, bad cop.

I've never felt freer than when I roar through the streets on my bike. That's right, I've owned this baby for years now, and only Minka knows. We reserve garage space under aliases for both our bikes and switch it up every few months. That is probably overkill, especially where I'm concerned, because up until recently, few people gave a shit about me or my hobbies. Again, that has been the goal all along. There are so many sayings about it always being the quiet one, yet the Gavinos apparently didn't put much stock in that. *Maybe they should read more memes.*

I've been on the road for about twenty minutes and slow as I spot the dirt road up ahead. Our rendezvous point is right at the edge of the city on land owned by Lucian Quinn. He is connected enough as the son-in-law of Lee Jacks for us to keep an eye on, and distant enough for none of the Gavinos or Morettis to be patrolling all his holdings. Especially in a sparsely populated area with the closest business being a couple of miles down the road. A light flashes three times in the distance, and I feel a wave of relief that we've both made it here safely once again. This is the last time for a few days unless there's some emergency. We both know we're pushing our luck, but it's so damned hard to stay away. Even though we don't normally see each other every day, something about having our wings clipped has made us both so incredibly restless. Min particularly. She's used to living with boundaries and security, but still, this is very different.

I take two steps forward when I get off the bike before I'm pulled into a tight embrace. I return the hug, feeling my eyes water. No matter where I go, the arms holding me will always be my home. "Damn, I was getting worried. What took you so long? Let me guess, standing around wringing your hands in indecision? Afraid Marco would need you to help him to the toilet for another round?"

"Min." I laugh as I pull away. "He's been really sick. I told you I shouldn't have added the anchovies."

She grimaces before adding, "It was likely the mineral oil. My grandma Francis used it as a laxative."

My mouth drops open in horror. "You told me it was okay to substitute for olive oil. You said, 'oil is oil, dummy.' Oh my God, do you think it's because I used the mineral oil that I remove my makeup with?" I'm pacing in the dark now as images of Marco's dead body float through my head. "I should have never listened to you. Shit, you don't know how to cook."

"For fuck's sake, Becky, calm down," she says dryly. I have no clue why, but she always calls me Becky when she's teasing me. I spin around and flip her off. I'll admit, it's not that effective, considering we can barely see each other, but it makes me feel better. She puts a hand on my shoulder and gives it a comforting squeeze. "I promise, Ni, he'll be fine. Yes, it was kind of an evil thing to do, but we had no idea it would cause such... distress. And we're talking about Marco Moretti here. If poisoning him didn't take him out, then I doubt mineral oil is going to do much to slow him down. Just think of it as an in-home colonic. They are all the rage these days, you know. A person could easily lose ten pounds depending on how full of shit they are. And in his case—yeah—he should be good for at least that."

"Min." I laugh despite myself. "I hope you're right. Otherwise, my ass is in big trouble when I get back."

From seemingly out of nowhere, a bright light shines in my eyes. I blink frantically, just before I'm pulled to the ground. "Fuck," Minka hisses. "Keep your head down. Someone's here."

"Indeed, they are, Sugar Lump," drawls a faintly amused voice. *It can't be.*

"Nic," I hear Minka groan incredulously. "He must have followed me. Shit."

"Actually, we both did," says someone just to my right. "And, Belle, you're correct about your ass being in big trouble. Only the time is now instead of later."

I don't want to stand. No, I'd rather stay low and crawl out of here, but Minka has no such qualms. Instead, she pops up like a Jack-in-the-box sounding very self-righteous for someone in the wrong. *Well, depending on how you look at it.* "This is a new low even for you, Nicole. What's next, sniffing my underwear? Talk about an invasion of privacy."

It appears I'm the only one still huddling on the ground. Pride demands that I at least look as if I have a set of balls. *Not that I do—or even want a pair, but... oh, fuck it.* The light that temporary blinded us has been lowered, and I can now easily make out a smirking Nic, a scowling Minka, and a blank-faced Marco. The last one is the worst. He might not be the most expressive guy, but this somber version is downright scary. *That's just your guilt talking.* "Give me a break," Nic mutters in response to Minka's tirade. "You're in the wrong, and you know it. If you must get yourself killed, then have at it, sweetheart, but don't drag innocent people into your insanity." He points in my direction before adding, "You have your friend here crawling down a building to meet you in a deserted field at midnight. That's crazy enough, but toss in the fact that there have been multiple murders lately, with a chunk of them involving Gavinos, and your crazy level goes right to insanely stupid. And how in the hell have you managed to get out of the compound without detection?"

"Oh, fuck you," Minka snarls. "You have no clue what you're talking about. Don't get pissy with me because you're too much of a pussy to do anything without written permission. Oh, and they don't make a security system that I can't defeat—obviously."

"Enough," Marco snaps out, and there is instant silence. I hear him sigh loudly, and strangely enough, it's comforting. *Well, that and the fact he doesn't simply shoot them both.* "This constant fucking bickering between you two is getting old. And this isn't the time for it. So shut the fuck up." The urge to smile is strong, but he takes care of that when he looks at me, then pointedly at my bike. "Unlike Nic, I don't think Minka led you astray. No, considering how adeptly you climb walls and handle that bike, you're no stranger to this level of duplicity. But why, Nina? I've brought you to *my* home to keep you safe. We have additional security to keep *you* fucking safe from who the fuck knows is the enemy. So other than sheer, reckless stupidity and selfishness, why?"

I feel like a five-year-old being taken to task by her father, and what's even worse, he's right. I'm surprised Minka hasn't jumped down his throat by now, but she's remained unusually quiet. I glance in her direction to make sure Nic doesn't have her in a choke hold, but there is no physical contact between them. They are, however, silently glaring at each other. I decide to go with as much truth as I can, figuring it'll sound more convincing. I clear my throat and summon the nerve to make full eye contact. *Crap, he's enraged.* It's there in his narrowed eyes and pursed lips. If I thought I could get away, I'd hop on my bike and make a run for it, but there is no way that's happening. "The first night I was at your apartment, I couldn't reach Minka. And we never go to bed without checking in. I tried her for hours and left countless messages, but nothing. I fell asleep and woke up after midnight. When I saw that she still hadn't responded, I knew something had to be wrong, so I let myself out and went to get my bike. I was about a mile from the Moretti compound when she texted to let me know that Nic had taken her phone, and she'd stolen it back when he was asleep." I put my hands on my hips, angry that he's made me out to be the bad guy here when Nic caused this.

"What are you talking about?" Nic chimes in. "I never took her phone." He holds his hands up when Marco looks at him questioningly. "Man, I swear, I haven't touched any of her shit. The only way that would happen is if you ordered it." Then he turns to Minka. "Why the fuck would you tell her that? Are you trying to start shit? In case you haven't noticed, we have enough problems without playing games with each other."

Minka reaches out and shoves against his chest as she snarls, "Would it have been better if I'd said, 'hey sorry, Ni, I was busy fucking Nic and missed your call?' My bad."

Whoa, so didn't see that coming. Nic, really? Tension fills the air as we all shift nervously on our feet. Well, everyone except Marco. He says absolutely nothing for a full, nail-biting minute. "Nic, call Jake and tell him to pick up these bikes. I'll take Nina with me, and you can take Minka." Oh shit. I haven't seen this version of Marco before.

"Hey, man," Nic says uneasily.

He glances at Nic for only a moment. "Call Jake and tell him to pick up these bikes." Then he turns to me. "Are you ready?" he asks me in a voice so deathly still and polite that it's almost eerie. Even Minka has been silenced. He holds the flashlight, and I follow him quietly through the woods to where the Escalade is parked in a clearing. He opens my door and walks around to the other side.

"Marco," I begin, having no idea what I plan to say but desperately wanting to break the heavy silence between us.

"Not now, Nina," he says shortly as he turns the ignition and swings the SUV around in the other direction. I open my mouth to make another attempt at conversation, but one look at his stiff profile stops me. *Nina. He called me Nina.* Twice. I've never seen him like this. I fear that I've lost someone who was more important to me than I realized. I flash back to those times when he showed up at my apartment to ask me out. He'd lean against the doorframe and flash me that cocky grin. The one that made my heart skip and my chest tight. I'd say something insulting, he'd laugh, and we'd spend another few minutes trading barbs before he'd either take his leave or make up some excuse to come inside. I acted as if I hated it when, secretly, it gave me a ridiculous glow for days afterward. I didn't want to be one of those women who swooned at the feet of a man who could have anyone he wanted. But dammit, even though I knew I wasn't special to him, that was what I felt, if for no other reason than he didn't chase women. He doesn't have to. Yet for over a year, he's shown up, time after time, with no sign of stopping. My willpower was almost nonexistent a week ago when he came for me. He could have probably gotten lucky that night without even buying me dinner first. He excites, confuses, and challenges me. But most of all, he tempts me beyond reason. God, I want him. I've written those very words hundreds of times before in my books, but I've never felt them—never really got them until him. And as much as I want slow and sweet, I also want him to fuck me until I stop thinking so damn much and just feel. I've always liked being in control of my life, but frankly, it's exhausting. *I just want to feel. I want to let go and have him take over my pleasure. Take control of me.* I came so close to orgasm simply from his kisses and touch a week ago, so I know it would be incredible with him. And that's what I want.

Desperately.

It's ironic that I finally admit the hard truth to myself, only to realize that the opportunity with Marco is gone. Because even if he can forgive everything I've done tonight, will he ever forget it? The underlying attraction between us has always been the cornerstone of our relationship, but I have a sick feeling in my stomach that everything has changed. I'm no longer the innocent he believed me to be. *Does that make me fair game?* That question haunts me as we near his apartment. One way or another, he'll answer it for me tonight, and I have no idea if I'm strong enough to survive his brand of reply.

7

Marco

I'm no longer furious. I've surpassed that. Hell, I'm not sure what I am. Stunned. Bewildered. All right, a little pissed. And strangely, a whole lot horny. The urge to pull the Escalade over and fuck Nina is almost more than I can bear. But first, I'd like to spank that ass for what she's put me through tonight. Seeing her fly through the streets on that damn sports bike was both the hottest thing I've ever seen—and the most terrifying. I had serious doubts that it was even her when she came roaring out of the parking garage on that death trap. Had it not been for the trackers I placed in the soles of all her shoes, I wouldn't have followed her. Nic had been just as skeptical. Granted, we knew she was a bit of a wild card and had more strength than expected. She had Langdon on the ground and under her control within seconds. Clearly, she picked up a thing or two from living with the Gavinos—self-preservation and survival being the most obvious skills. I had no clue what she was capable of. She's a beautifully confusing puzzle I have to put together, but I'm deathly afraid I don't have the patience or control to do it slowly.

I pull up in front of my building and leave the Escalade running.

Wade steps out of the shadows, but one look at my face kills whatever smart comment he was on the verge of uttering. Instead, he nods at Nina as she walks slowly around the vehicle and stops a few feet away. I motion for her to precede me and grind my teeth as my eyes go directly to her ass as she moves toward the elevators. Then swear to fuck, according to the sign, they're temporarily out of order. *Go fuck yourself and use the stairs.* It's a special kind of hell that has me following those swinging hips up dozens of steps. The way those pants cling to that round, juicy ass should be illegal. The things I'm dreaming of doing to it probably are. But I'm strong, and I could have made it—if only she didn't stumble and fall back into me. "Whoops, sorry," she whispers.

And that's it.

I lose it. Despite previous assurances to both her and myself that I'd spend hours driving her crazy, I'm all over her. I lift her up the next step to the landing and back her into the corner. Then my mouth is on hers, and my hands are everywhere. Like a predator, I'm entirely focused on her to the exclusion of everything else. I growl low in my throat as I yank both her top and bra down in one move. When her tits bounce free, my mouth latches on one, and my teeth mark it. She cries out, and I pause, wondering how the fuck I'll stop if that's what she wants. But I know I will regardless of the cost. I've never taken a woman against her will, and the one in my arms means more to me than any others ever have. "Belle? Tell me right now."

She climbs me, literally grabs my neck, and hoists her body up before wrapping her legs around my waist. Then she makes an irritated grunting noise as she sticks her other tit in my face. "If you stop, I'll kill you, Moretti."

So hot. Thank fuck. I vaguely recognize that I'm not only claiming her, but I'm also fucking marking her. *I never do that.* And she's doing the same as I nip and suck every inch of exposed body I can get to. "I've gotta fuck you, Belle. Can't stop. Hold on to me." She grips me tighter, and I wedge her closer to the wall for support while I unzip and lower my jeans and boxer briefs. She's wiggling so much in my arms that for a moment I damn near panic, thinking she's trying to get down. But when I glance down, she's attempting to push her own pants down and having a harder time since they're so tight. "Straighten." She immediately stops what she's doing and unlocks her legs from my waist to dangle at my sides. I put one hand against her back and use the other to slide the pants down. "Kick," I add and grin when one of her shoes falls off allowing me to completely free one leg. *Perfect.*

"Condom," she adds, and again I'm shifting her around as I dig for my wallet in my back pocket. The juggling act has gotten so detailed and comical that I know it would be easier to go up a few more flights of stairs to my apartment, but I don't think either of us is willing to be denied another two minutes. So she opens the condom while I toss my wallet aside, and considering how many I've used in my life, I have it on in seconds. My hands are on her ass now as I hold her suspended above the tip of my cock. I lower her just an inch, and we both groan at the initial penetration. "Teamwork makes the dream work," she moans, and I lower my head into the crook of her neck as I release a ragged laugh.

"Fucking right it does, baby," I hiss as I lower her hips while thrusting upward until I'm buried to the hilt inside her hot, wet warmth. My usual finesse has deserted me as I take her hard and fast. But goddamn, she's right there with me. Her nails are digging deep through the material of my shirt, and I can only marvel at the strength in those petite legs as she raises and lowers herself onto my cock as if unable to wait to take more inside her.

"Marco," she cries out before lowering a hand between us and rubbing her clit. "Can't wait . . . I need... now."

At the sight of her taking what she wants, my balls draw up tight, and I know I'm only seconds away from blowing. Sweat is pouring down my back and trickling from my brow as I begin reciting baseball statics in my head. *Anything* to distract me from the way she's grinding against me while working her nub furiously. I've never had to resort to it before, but I've never wanted anyone the way I do her. *2017 World Series. Astros win first title ever. Dodgers lose in game seven.* She's yelling my name now, the sound of her voice and our bodies slapping together echoing off the stairwell like a scene from a porn movie. *Two-run homer by George Springer. Wait, what did she just say? No, I couldn't have heard that right.*

"Will you fucking slap my ass, Moretti?" she snaps impatiently.

I pause, my hips freezing with my dick buried to the hilt. I squeeze the area in question. "You want me to slap this?"

She stares up at me, blinking owlishly before narrowing her eyes and wiggling her hips. "Stop being such a prude, Moretti. If I'm going to be fucked like this, then I want the whole experience."

Fuck my life. Baseball can't save me now. A cold shower and Nic walking around naked couldn't put this fire out. I flip around, putting my back against the wall and exposing hers fully, then I free one hand and slap that ass. She tenses when I make contact, but I feel her pussy contracting around me. *She's into it. Her body is damn near applauding.* I switch to the other cheek, and that's it, she's coming so hard I have no choice but to go with her. Her pussy won't allow anything else. She's greedily milking me dry. "Ahhh, fuck," I roar as my vision grows dim for a moment.

"Don't drop me." I jerk, holding her tightly to me, and we both hiss as my cock slides deep once again. *Hmm, round two...* "Don't even think about it, Moretti." She giggles as she snuggles closer for a moment. "I'd rather the few people in this building who haven't already seen or heard us to remain that way. Plus"—she winces— "I think I've got road rash on my back."

I'm a complete asshole. I press a gentle kiss to her forehead, then one to the tip of her nose before reluctantly separating us. When her legs are steady, I pull my shirt off and use it clean her up until we reach my place. She appears almost shy now as I pull her pants back up and rearrange her top before righting my own clothes. She mumbles her thanks, then takes a few steps forward. But there's no way I'm letting her leave without making something clear. I sense that if I wait even the few minutes it will take to reach my apartment, it will be too late. "Belle," I say softly as I put my hand on her arm. She turns back to look at me questioningly, but I see what she's trying to hide. *Doubt. Insecurity.* But it's the last one that slays me—hope. *Fuck, she owns me. Has no clue, but she does.* I cup her face, brushing my thumb tenderly over her swollen lips. "That was amazing. Better than I ever dreamed, and believe me, baby, I've thought of little else since I met you."

She looks down at her feet before glancing back up. "But... I'm just... me. You can have anyone you want, so you can't possibly—"

"You want to know what makes you different, Belle?" *I've fucked nameless girls, but they haven't been who I've wanted. And I never want to go back.* When she nods, I lean down until we're eye to eye before saying slowly and clearly, "You. Belong. To. Me. Haven't we both always known that?"

Being the stubborn little shit that she is, I can see an objection forming. But then she surprises me by shrugging. "I suppose we have." My surprise turns to shock when she spins around and runs up the steps, stopping at the next landing. She flashes me an impish smile that's purely a mixture of angel and devil. "Doesn't mean I have to like it, though, Moretti." She leaves me there, pretty much with my dick in my hand and my mouth hanging open. For a guy like me, I all but declare my undying love for her, and she walks away? I'm almost pissed until I see her rub her ass, undoubtedly sore from the few smacks I gave it. Then she winks at me in a way that tells me she's more than happy to be mine. *God help me, what have I gotten myself into?* Somehow, I think being mafia has now officially become the easier part of my life. Surviving the little spitfire whose finger I'm wrapped around is gonna be the real challenge.

Nina

Feeling such a warm and fuzzy glow, I don't think anything can bring me down. That is, until I throw open the door from the stairwell to Marco's floor and come face to face with a grinning Jake. "Well, hello, sweet pea. I wondered when you two would make it up those last steps. It was becoming quite challenging to keep the other residents from crashing your... party. There's an irate woman downstairs with blue hair and a possessed poodle according to Wade. She's threatened to have him singing soprano by shoving her cane in a certain orifice."

I don't need a mirror to know I'm blushing furiously. My face is on fire from within. When something touches my hip, I whirl, expecting to see Wade. But luckily, it's Marco. And I can't believe my eyes. *He's embarrassed.* The ladies' man extraordinaire shoves both hands in his pockets and rocks back on his heels as he looks everywhere except at his grinning cousin. It probably doesn't help that he's holding his shirt —the one he used on me—instead of wearing it. Obviously, he caught the last part of our conversation because he says, "Appreciate the... um assistance, bro."

"No problem, man." Jake nods. "Didn't mean to come across as a creeper. But when there was still no sign of you two, we got a little concerned. After we located you, we locked the area down. Didn't want anyone catching you unawares." Lowering his voice, he adds, "I—um, will also take care of any footage from cameras in the stairwell." *Oh my God, why didn't I think of that? Hey Nina, saw your ass on YouTube... literally.* Marco extends a fist, and they do the whole bro gratitude thing before Jake walks to the door of the apartment, unlocks it, and disarms the security system. "Just finished making a sweep of the place, so you're good to go. Let me know if you need anything." Before he moves away, he pauses next to me to add, "Sorry about the teasing, Nina. But it's sort of a rite of passage. For what it's worth, we wouldn't bother unless we considered you one of us."

I'm strangely touched by the explanation. I take them both by surprise when I briefly hug the other man. After all, I owe him for protecting not only Marco's privacy but mine as well. Jake laughs at Marco's possessive growl before disappearing down the hallway. "He's a nice guy," I say truthfully. "You're lucky to be surrounded by so many family members."

"Mostly, yeah," Marco says as he walks into the kitchen. A few moments later, he returns with a bottle of water for each of us. He absently pushes a stray hair behind my ear. My bun from earlier has long since fallen victim to our stairwell romp. "There are times it's been both a blessing and a curse, but they've always had my back. There are some within the family who aren't as... intuitive as others. But I trust all of them with my life. And yours, Belle."

I take the bottle that he extends and twist the cap off. After downing half the bottle, I wait as he does the same. "Even now, with all that's happened? Hits on people all around you, including an attempt on your own life? Has any of those events shaken your faith in your own family?" He runs a hand through his hair and absently rubs his temple. He's so exhausted that I regret bringing up something so heavy now. He's a very shrewd man. If I've thought it, then there is no way he hasn't. And for a family as close as the Morettis, suspicion within their folds would be torturous to even contemplate. I place my hand on his forearm and give it an understanding squeeze. "Forget I asked. I don't know about you, but I'm exhausted. I'm going to take a quick shower before bed."

I've made it a few steps when he says quietly, "I don't know what to believe anymore, Belle, and I fucking hate it more than you can imagine. Franklin and Frankie Jr. were one thing, but the shit that's followed has me kind of freaked the fuck out. I have no answers for any of that— not even an inkling—and I don't know why. I can't help but wonder if it's because there are no clues or simply that I don't want to see what could well be in my own backyard."

I mull over his words as he moves away. "Why do you see my stepfather and stepbrother's deaths differently? Does it mean that you know who killed them, or is it that you don't care?"

He freezes, literally turns to stone.

What is going on?

Does he know more than he's told me?

Even though he's facing away from me, I can sense his indrawn breath. Can practically hear his brain whirling frantically. The entire thing lasts no more than twenty or thirty seconds, but the doubt it casts in its wake will remain much longer. His expression when he turns to me shows nothing out of the ordinary, and it's as if I've imagined the whole thing. Even if he does have an inkling, we're talking a probable mafia hit, and other than my last name, I'm very much an outsider and not privy to that information. As he's told me many times before, it's not safe for us to even be having a conversation pertaining to family business. I expect him to shrug my questions off, but he closes the distance between us and pulls me into his arms. My face rests in the crook of his neck and his hands smooth up and down my spine. "I have nothing concrete, Belle. Frankie's interests and side activities put him on the radar of a lot of people—none of them good. He drew attention not only to himself but also to all the Gavinos. And that's just the little I know or have heard from various sources. Probably plenty hasn't been uncovered yet. So yeah, I'm not exactly shocked that something happened to him. And even though he knew his son's faults, Franklin would have laid down his life to protect him. Pretty much figure it went down that way."

What he says makes sense, and it's along the lines of what I've thought as well. But it *feels* wrong, in a way that I can't lay my finger on. It's been a hell of a day, and we're both wiped. My already active imagination is no doubt running on overdrive because of it. I pause at his bedroom door, the one I've taken as my own, and wonder if he plans to join me. But he continues toward the guest bathroom, and I swallow my disappointment at the thought of spending another night alone. *So much for his speech about me belonging to him.* "Good night," I call out to his retreating back.

I'm already across the threshold when suddenly he's back, appearing confused. "What's with the brushoff?"

Well, that makes two of us. Because I must surely resemble a deer in headlights. "I... what are you talking about?"

He closes his eyes for a moment, pinching the bridge of his nose before opening them. "I thought it went without saying that you would do whatever you do before bed and meet me in the spare room."

"Why would I do that?" I ask slowly. I realize I'm tired, but he's making zero sense to me.

At my question, he has that same awkward look he had earlier with Jake. "Er... I know how you feel about my... bed." He releases a pained hiss before adding, "And fuck, I'm on the same page now. Until it can be replaced, we sleep in there," he says, pointing toward the other room. "Just thought you might like some privacy first, that's all."

Could he be any more adorable? I nod and mumble my thanks before escaping to the bathroom so he won't see my sappy expression. He seriously rocked my world in the stairwell, but I expected nothing less in that area. Yet what has transpired since is unexpected. Not only verbally laying claim to me but also being sweet and understanding. If this is the real Marco, then I've been a fool to hold out this long. I've undressed and am stepping into the shower when I see the faint pink prints on my ass. *Oh my God.* I asked—no—demanded he spank me. He was so shocked he almost dropped me. *Where did that even come from?* I was so caught up in the moment, so close to the most amazing orgasm ever, yet I needed a little push. A nudge to roar across the finish line. And seemingly from nowhere, I knew that was it. The only thing to catapult me into the great coital bliss. *Boy, did it ever.* He may think I'm a freak now, but the whole experience was strangely liberating. I gave myself over to another person, trusting them with not only my body but a big chunk of my heart as well. I can either have a panic attack and retreat or embrace it, knowing I may get hurt in the end. But at least I'll be living my life.

I'm practically asleep on my feet when I tiptoe into the guestroom and pause next to the bed. Marco has left one lamp on, and that feels like an unspoken welcome of sorts. His eyes are closed, and I'm almost sure he's asleep. A startled squeak leaves my mouth when he suddenly lifts the cover without a word, but I climb awkwardly in next to him. "Thanks," I murmur. The need to fill the silence is too much. "Jake most certainly knew what we were... you know, doing. And poor Wade was under attack from an old lady and a blue poodle. Wait. Maybe it was a blue lady and a young poodle." My brow furrows, and I try to remember the conversation. "Oh well, I'm not sure. But either way, he deserved it for teasing you about your stomach... issues." *I haven't even asked how he's feeling. Real nice, Nina. He spanks your ass, but you can't be bothered to inquire about the state of his? So selfish. Way to worry about number one.* My thoughts are interrupted when the bed begins shaking. *Is he having a bad dream? Medical emergency?* "Are you all right?" I ask, wishing he hadn't turned the light off now. My hands move over his chest, before finding his face. His mouth definitely appears to be turned upward.

He hugs me tighter, and I return the embrace, still having no idea what is going on with him. "Belle?" He pauses until he hears me grunt a muffled response against his chest. "My ass is fine." He lowers his hand and squeezes one of my cheeks before adding, "And I'm more than happy to focus on yours. You could say, it's number one with me as well."

My mind is buzzing in confusion. *How?* "Um... that's good," I mumble uncertainly. "Glad to hear we're on the same page. I think."

He chuckles once again, and I'm beginning to think he's one of those people who gets silly when they're tired. I wouldn't have guessed it, but how well do you ever really know someone? "You realize you said all that about my ass—and yours—out loud, right? The part about being selfish and wondering about my ass health? Granted, it was a little muddled since you were speaking so fast, but I think I caught most of it. Fuck, I certainly hope so because it was hilarious."

"Oh shit," I moan in horror. *Not again.* "I've developed a bad habit of talking to myself since I work from home. With no co-workers, the only human interaction I get is with—me. Normally, that wouldn't be a big deal, but I blurt things out at times without even knowing it. Like the time I thought to myself that my neighbor should burn the sweatpants she's always wearing. Unfortunately, I thought it verbally while she was a few inches in front of me. Things became awkward between us after that. It had been a huge relief when she relocated to South Carolina with her job. Otherwise, I feared she'd have strangled me with those horrid, pink pants one night while I was sleeping." *Talk about dying an ugly death.* He's laughing hysterically again, and I inwardly groan, knowing I've shared something else without intending to. I dig my elbow in his ribs and enjoy his grunt of pain. "Oh, shut up already, Moretti."

He pulls back for a moment, and I feel his eyes on me in the dark. "I'm just teasing you, Belle. It's all a part of your beautifully quirky, sweet, and unique personality. There is absolutely nothing about you I'd change." With impressive accuracy, his mouth lands on mine, and he kisses me leisurely, almost tenderly before moving onto his back and settling me in the crook of his arm. *Marco, the snuggle bunny. Who'd have thunk it?* I marvel at how perfectly we fit together. How easy this transition from kinda friends to lovers has been thus far. I know instinctively that it's no accident. He's made it this way. To get me out of my head and trust where he leads. If this is an example of what's to come, then I couldn't be happier.

I'll look back in the days ahead and wonder if that one line jinxed everyone and everything around me.

8

Marco

I awake to a warm body in my arms and an ass pressed against my hard dick. Certainly not the worst way to begin a day, but haven't I learned a lesson about letting women stay the night? That kind of shit leads to mixed signals and expectations—when all I really want is a little pussy to calm the beast within—or in this case, the one below. *Well, too late now. Might as well get off before I get her out. I'll even be a gentleman and wake her with a bang.* I'm still half-asleep when I spread her legs and position her ankles over my shoulders. She's yet to say anything. If not for her faint snores, I'd be checking her for signs of life. *Wtf?* She's wearing panties, which is unusual. And they're a little on the granny side, so I chalk up another oddity. *Pity fuck?* I disregard that notion immediately. I've never fucked anyone I wasn't attracted to. It takes some work, but I remove her bad choice of underwear. *When in doubt, ladies, go without.*

The visibility isn't that great, but my hand tells me the lawn hidden beneath the cotton wood-killers is nicely maintained. I sniff and growl approvingly. I ease her folds aside and take a long lick up her slit. *Fuck yeah.* I'm not one to brag, but if eating pussy were an Olympic sport, I'd take home the gold *every* fucking time. It doesn't surprise me to hear her begin to moan, nor am I shocked when she buries a hand in my hair and yanks. *I need to get that shit buzzed off. Fucking hurts.* No, neither of these two things are unusual. But what does give me pause—no, freezes me in place—is when the woman attached to the pussy I'm enjoying croaks out, "Marco, that better be you down there." Followed by, "Oh. My. GOD."

Whoa, the fuck is going on? Then it all comes back to me. I suck her clit into my mouth as she impatiently pushes her hand against my skull. She responds in a mixture of gibberish and moans. Yeah, I know it's a dick move considering I thought she was someone else only moments before, but I can't resist. I'm in the mood to play. The more impatient her moans and movements become, the slower I go. *This is my show, baby, so get used to it.* The little minx actually tries to touch herself as I circle her clit but don't directly touch it. *No, no. Bad girls get punished, not rewarded.* I'm half afraid she'll snap my neck or choke me with her thighs in frustration. *Death by an angry pussy. I can deal with it.* "What do you want, Belle? Tell me, and I'll give it to you." *Some version at least.*

"You... inside me," she gasps as her hips lift, and her body shakes. *Ohhh, great answer. Ask and you shall receive.* I trail my index finger through her wetness and grin when her breath catches. I push the tip of it inside her pussy before pulling it out. Pretty sure I hear her teeth grinding, but she doesn't say anything. I toss in a little distraction by pinching her clit between the fingers of my other hand before stealthily moving to her lonely and no doubt virgin ass. I press my finger against the pucker gently but firmly. All movement stops, her body is taut and utterly still. She voices no objections and appears to be awaiting my next move. I pinch her clit harder, and she cries out just as I slide my finger in to the knuckle. "I... Marco, stop," she says with uncertainty. I do as she asks, going no deeper. Yet I keep the pressure on her clit so she has no choice but to accept the sensations that stimulating both areas brings. She's absolutely soaking wet now.

Her mind may be resisting, but her body is on board. Hell, that's no different than most things in life. Even though I'm intent on teasing her, the decision to try something new is ultimately hers to make, and I'll never force it on her. So—I wait. When she rocks her hips, forcing me deeper, I smile. "That's my girl," I say as I slip the rest of the way inside while continuing to work her pussy. She's so responsive. So fucking perfect. My cock is as hard as nails, but I push the discomfort to the side to give her what she needs. When she's close, I move away from her clit and push my finger into her pussy. She's shaking so much now, I almost stop. But her moans cannot be mistaken for anything other than pleasure. She'll kick my ass if I let off without giving her an orgasm. The sensation of fullness is too much for her to bear, and she explodes, screaming my name, along with Jesus, God, Mary, Joseph, and even Santa and his reindeer. She comes for a second time when she reaches Rudolph.

Understandable, he's everyone's favorite.

Then she collapses in a heap of heaving, satisfied, exhausted woman. But I'm not done with her yet. I've been good long enough. "Flip over onto your stomach, Belle." She mutters something but does as I ask. If she's expecting a backrub, she's in for a surprise. I quickly grab a condom from the nightstand and roll it on before moving back to her. I plant a knee on either side of her hips before nudging her ass with my dick.

"Ain't happening, buddy," she tosses out, without raising her head. "Move on, nothing to see here." I chuckle despite myself. Humor hasn't been something that's occurred during sex in the past, but I find it both sexy and endearing. And so very Belle. I pop first one cheek and then the other, enjoying the sight of my handprint on her white skin. She mumbles something else but doesn't object. I nudge her legs apart enough to settle my cock at the entrance of her pussy, then grunt in bliss when I slide home easily. "Mmm," she purrs. And God, that sound out of her mouth about me? About what I'm doing to her? Best fucking sound to hear. *She's so fucking perfect.*

This position is impossibly deep and tight, which is why I love it. Also, the added visual of my dick disappearing between the cheeks of her ass is damn near euphoric. She tries to push back, but I place a hand on her shoulder to keep her immobile. That's my Belle, always trying to top from the bottom. I'm sure I'll hear plenty of complaints later, but her cries of pleasure tell the truth. I grit my teeth, feeling my balls tighten in an embarrassingly short amount of time. *2016 World Series. Cubs win in the seventh game.* This position is far too tempting, so I pull out and grin at her howl of outrage. "Relax, sweetheart, you'll get yours. Again." She gives an inelegant snort that turns into a hiss as she lands on her back and I pull her legs around my hips. I place one hand under her neck and the other under her ass and I drive back into her. I don't need to tell her to grip me tighter because her legs are damn near cutting me in two as she rides my cock. I usually prefer to avoid positions that are too intimate—and kissing is about as personal as you can get. But with her, I love sliding my tongue into her mouth as my cock mimics the movement in her pussy. I'm so fucking lost in her—at the moment, that crazy shit floats through my mind. *Two hearts that beat as one. My other half. The fucking wind beneath my wings. Maybe I should go back to baseball stats. Less confusing and not as likely to make my dick go limp with all the sappy thoughts.* We're in the home stretch now, racing at a frantic pace toward oblivion. Then I go deeper, grinding against her clit, and that's it. The sweet spot for both of us. I see stars. Go hot and cold, then back again within seconds. Feel my heart stop, then gallop damn near out of my chest.

"Marco," she moans. "So good. God, make it stop." *Yeah, baby, good is an understatement. I aim to please. Wait, what? Stop?*

I pull back so I can see her flushed face. Sweet Lord, she's crying. Tears are rolling down her cheeks. The heady afterglow suffers a damn near fatal blow to the gut. *Fuck, I hurt her. I thought she was with me.*

Goddamn, fuck.

I freeze, having no idea what to do or how to handle something like this. I've never hurt a woman before, and this is my Belle. I begin to ease slowly from her body, trying desperately to be as gentle as I can. "I'm so sorry, baby," I whisper. "What... where do you hurt? I'll call the doc. We have a woman on the payroll who will be here in like thirty. Or if you'd rather go to the emergency room, we can do that. Yeah, you're right, that's what we need to do. Hang tight, I'll have the car brought around."

"Are you high?" she asks in a voice full of confusion. "Why would I need a doctor? Oh no, you meant for you, didn't you? You're probably really dehydrated after the stomach issue, and I've been relentless." She shoves at my chest as she attempts to wiggle her way from under me. "I'll call Jake. He can carry you."

Now I'm the one who's bewildered. "Belle, I don't know what you're talking about. Would you settle down before you hurt yourself?"

She pauses, putting a hand on my cheek. "You're sick, honey. I didn't mean to, but I've fucked you—too much. Now, you need medical attention." She kisses my brow and again tries to get up. "You're really going to have to release me, Marco." When she presses her hand against my forehead as if checking me for a temperature, I get a strange lump in my throat. *Hell, maybe I am sick.* Out of all the women who've come and gone from my life—a few with the assistance of a restraining order—I've never had one who actually cared. I mean, there have been insane declarations of love and devotion, but not the kind Nina is showing me now. I've only gotten this from one woman, and she's legally obligated to put up with my stubborn ass. I need to stop this—now. I can't think straight when she's like this.

"Belle," I say in exasperation, "I'm fine. You're the one I'm concerned about. You told me to make it stop or something. I assumed that indicated a problem. I was simply repeating what you said, that's it. So how about we rewind, and you tell me exactly what made you say that?"

She wrinkles her nose in that adorable way that makes me want to fuck her—again. "I got nothing." She finally shrugs. "Oh, wait." She snaps her fingers. "I couldn't stop my orgasm. And you kept on rubbing that one spot." She reaches out and pats my hands as if to reassure me. "Don't get me wrong, it felt good, but I thought I was going to pass out. I've never come more than four times... and that was on my own. You know, stroking, then using my rabbit, a combination of both, and the final that gets you back from the edge. Other than the first, that one is the most important, don't you think? Otherwise, you're still all strung out, which isn't how you want to be after spending all that time getting off, know what I mean?" *Fuck my life. Why must she overshare?*

"Yeah, I get it." I nod absently as I ponder which way I'll fuck her next. It's not a question of if because, thanks to her masturbation chat, it's gotta happen before I leave this room. *Since she loves giving orders when she's horny, time for her to take the top spot.*

I'm pulling her closer, and she's giving me a look that's both wary and turned on when someone nearby clears their throat. Our heads swivel as one, and I dive for the covers, doing my best to make myself decent. Unfortunately, my sudden movement topples Nina, who ends up naked and indignant in the floor. "Marco," she cries out, then glances from our intruder to me with narrowed eyes. "Sorry," she says, "we're not auditioning for a threesome today. Kindly leave your key and a number where you can be reached in case of any STD updates in the future."

My mother looks down at Nina before raising a brow in my direction. "At least this one has a sense of humor and the ability to form sentences consisting of more than three words. Bravo, my darling boy, you're making progress."

Nina appears to have forgotten that she's still naked. Either that, or she's trying to prove a point to the woman she believes to be a former lover. I hold the blanket over my lap and toss a nearby pillow to Nina. She's going to want that soon. "Nina, this is my very rude mother, Angelica, who loves dropping in without warning. Mom, this is Nina Gavino, my... Belle." *That didn't sound awkward at all.* Nina squeaks, wrapping her arms around the pillow like a lifeline. Her face is so red, it looks as if she'll burst into flames at any moment.

My mother is surprised by the surname. No, shocked might be a better word. She's friendly with several of the Gavino wives, but she's very much a woman of the old mafia. Being cordial is one thing, but having your only son fuck the enemy is another. *I'm going to catch hell over this.* I love my mother—I absolutely worship her. She's a scary mix of angel and demon. She bows to no one, and that includes the men in our family. She's also probably the shrewdest person I know, other than my father. She walks over to Nina and extends a hand. "It's nice to meet you, Nina. I've heard of you, of course. I met your mother a few times through the years." She places her other hand over their clasped ones before adding, "She was a beautiful person, and I mourned her passing along with many others."

"Th—thank you, Mrs. Moretti," Nina says thickly, obviously still affected by the loss of her mother.

"Tsk, please call me Angelica, my dear. We don't stand on formality. You may not be a Moretti, but the Gavinos have been close allies for many years. And now with the loss of Franklin and your stepbrother, so much tragedy for one so young to bear."

Nina looks devastated, and I kick myself for leaving her on the fucking floor naked to endure this. This has gone on too fucking long. "Mom, could you please make yourself comfortable in the living room while Nina and I dress?" She knows me well enough to understand that my question isn't really a question at all.

"Oh, what was I thinking? Of course, darling. Nina, please forgive me for being so terribly rude." Nina nods, then sags weakly when my mother leaves, closing the door behind her.

"Oh my God," she groans as she buries her face in her hands. "Your mom caught us practically humping each other. And to make matters worse, I sat here like a dolt letting it all hang out." She lifts her head and turns to glare at me. "Why in the world didn't you do something sooner? I was clearly in shock, but what's your excuse?"

I toss the blanket aside and get to my feet, before stooping to help her up. "I have none," I say honestly. "I'm not used to this kind of unannounced drop-in. She usually calls or at the very least, comes later in the day. I was just as surprised as you were."

I reach over to kiss her, and she hand-blocks me. *The fuck?* "Don't even think about it. We can't be trusted, and you know that. If our body parts so much as touch, we'll be going at it like rabbits. Then your mom will barge in right as I demand you choke me or something similarly shocking. It's a risk we can't take."

I try, really, I do, but I can't contain my laughter. She, however, doesn't look amused at all. She crosses her arms over her chest as her foot taps furiously on the floor. "Er... sorry?" I murmur contritely.

"I'm going to use the shower in here because there's no way I'm going down the hall until I'm fully dressed." When I move in the direction of the bathroom, she grabs my arm, halting me. "Nope, you'll use your room. But before you shower, bring me my suitcase."

"*Gee, I thought I had at least a few weeks before the bossy, non-sex part of the relationship kicked in. Fucking Google sure lied about that one.*"

"Excuse me?" she says, putting her hands on her hips as she glares at me.

Oh shit, now I'm the one thinking out loud. Big problem for a man like me. Let's hope it's a weird thing that only she brings out. Considering she's typically not much of an exhibitionist, I'm betting she forgot about being butt naked. *Little hard for me to take her anger seriously when those luscious tits are only inches away. And that ass—the things I'm gonna do to it. Fuck me.* I give her the dumbest look I can muster, which isn't that tough since all the blood in my body has rushed south. "Just going over my to-do list for the day. Important mafia stuff and all that." *That ass of yours is number one, sweetheart.* "I'll go get those things you need now."

I give her my sweetest smile as I stroll past. And she gives me one in return, only hers is more of a full-body leer. "Oh, and baby?" I pause, taken aback by the endearment. She follows it up with a wink as she says, "You might want to cover that thing up. God willing, it looks a little different than it did the last time your mommy saw it." She places a fingertip on her chin as if pondering something of the utmost importance before adding, "Well, unless she was here for longer than we're aware of earlier."

Crash and burn, baby, crash and burn. We've got a total loss of manhood here.

Thanks for that, Mom.

I shake my head as I locate the pants I wore last night and put them on. "That was pure evil, Belle. Never mention a parental figure while my dick's hard. That's a hard limit."

"Of course, Mr. Moretti." As usual, she manages to get in the last word. *Well, maybe it's not so bad this time. I like that version of "Mr. Moretti." We can work with it—later.* "As long as you keep your mommy out of the bedroom while you're bumping uglies with me." *Ding, ding, winner by knockout!*

She's in the bathroom with the door shut before I can think of a response. *Hell, probably for the best. We'd be here all day trying to one-up each other.* I gather her things and leave them for her before showering and dressing. I'm sitting on the bed strapping on my ankle holster when my phone rings. I see my father's name and grin. "What's with you and Mom today? I promise I'm not feeling neglected."

There's silence before he says, "Glad to hear it, whatever the fuck you're talking about. But I need you at Cypher now. There's been an attempted hit on Ray Gavino. He's hanging on, but one of his guards is dead. Have Jake take Nina to the compound. She needs to be off-grid until we know more."

"Fuck. I'll be there in twenty," I mutter as I stand and make quick work of loading my second gun into the shoulder harness. With all the shit going on, I should probably be wearing a vest as well, but there's no time. I stride to the front door, texting Jake as I go. He meets me in the hallway as I hit send, and I quickly bring him up to date on Ray. "Listen, I need for you to take Nina to Tony's."

He looks behind him before lowering his voice and saying, "The kid is with me. He was having a rough time of it this morning, and Wade didn't know how to deal. Let me take him by the office and then I'll drop Nina off. Too soon in the game for him to know the setup at the compound."

"Son, I'll take Nina. I have two guards downstairs. She'll be safer with me right now than one of your men." Fuck, my mother has always moved around as quiet as a ninja. It's damn unsettling—and more than a little impressive. "Go," she prompts when I appear undecided. "For God's sake, I managed to keep you alive for eighteen years. I think I can handle your friend."

I don't want to, but she's right. No women have been targeted, so in theory, Nina is safer with Mom. And I have no time left to ponder it. I mutter my thanks and take off at a fast clip. I'm in my vehicle and halfway to Cypher before it hits me. I forgot to say goodbye to Nina. Not only that, but I also left her alone with my mother without warning. *I'm fucked. If some nutjob doesn't kill me, she likely will.* I've always known relationships are dangerous for men like me, but I've broken my rules at the worst time possible. Another hit that we're not responsible for. I can't relax my guard for a moment. Because now, Nina is mine, one of *my* people to protect. And I know if anything happens to her, I'll never recover from it. I became jaded to death long ago. Yeah, it bothers me, and it fucking sucks for those left behind, but it's the reality in my world—both of them. And even worse, innocents die a hell of a lot more than the bad guys. Collateral damage. Sacrifice a few to save many. *Blah, blah.* I've heard that dozens of times in varying forms. Simply put, everyone is expendable to someone. You just have to hope the someone who wants rid of you is never in a position to call the shots.

I push it all aside as I slow to make the first of a series of turns that leads to the entrance to Cypher. Everything else must take a back seat because I'm not only Moretti mafia here, I'm Marco Moretti, FBI agent assigned to a joint task force with the ATF and DEA. Oh, and my father is not only the head of the Moretti family, but he's also the SAC or Special Agent-in-Charge of the North Carolina FBI Organized Crimes Division. And this is where things get complicated. It's my job to let the small fish go in favor of the much bigger catch. As fucked up as it sounds, it also gives the Morettis a certain amount of immunity from law enforcement, with ironclad agreements in place that both ex-family members, Lee and Tony, are exempt from any past, present, or future actions. It's tricky and requires finesse and not a small number of downright brawls between the power players on all ends, but it's worked so far. Only now, a new player in town is causing upheaval, and none of us can rest until we find and eliminate them. After that, I'll go back to doing my job and trying to figure out how the fuck I can keep Nina when I've done nothing but lie to her—and that's not something I can ever change.

Nina

He is so dead when I get my hands on him. I hope he enjoyed the sex because it's over—maybe that is a tad drastic...

Apparently, there was an emergency, and he's taken off. Would the two minutes it would have taken to tell me this himself really have made a difference? And there's been another hit on a Gavino. Minka's father, Ray. I want to call her, but since I'll see her in person soon, I decide to wait. I have no idea if Nic told her, and I certainly don't want to do it over the phone.

Jake gave me a sympathetic look before discreetly dragging his finger across his neck while Angelica's back was turned. He arrived a few moments ago to walk us down to where a black Mercedes waits at the curb. Two men hopped out of the front when we approached and Jake fist-bumped the rather large one called Moose before repeating the gesture with the thin, wiry one called Jimmy. "You know the drill. Make sure you check in when you reach the compound. Keep your eyes open and take care of the bosses' ladies."

I see Angelica's mouth tighten slightly at Jake's inclusion of me, but it's gone so quickly, I wonder if I imagined it. "You got it, chief." Moose nods agreeably as he opens one of the back doors for Angelica. Jimmy motions for me to follow him to the other side and does the same for me. Even though the Mercedes is roomy inside, it still puts me in very close quarters with Marco's mother. As uncomfortable as she makes me, I can't help but admire her. She's a beautiful woman, one who could easily pass for someone my age. Her hair is the same shade as Marco's. It appears to be about waist length, and she's wearing it in an elegant French twist. She's taller than me with a trim, athletic figure, which is shown to perfection in tight skinny jeans, black knee-high boots, and a cowl-neck sweater. I was proud of my mom when she attended my school events, but Angelica's the type of mother who all the kids would stare at. Mine was pretty, but Angelica is perfection. *And she saw me naked, sprawled on her son's floor about thirty minutes ago.*

I'm startled from my reverie when she says, "I never thanked you for saving my son. I know you were the one who found him. You could have easily chosen not to get involved, but you took the lesser-traveled path. For that, you have my gratitude."

"That's really not necessary. I'm sure anyone would have done the same." *Especially if they were female.* A picture pops in my head of Kathy Bates in *Misery*. Poor Marco could have ended up tied to a bedpost. *I think we'll try that next. Hot guy at my mercy. Begging. Pleading. Promising me anything to release him. Oh shit, back away from the light, Nina. His mother is right here. Don't blush, don't blush—she'll know.* God, I hope we're close to our destination. But I've only been to the compound once, so I have no idea.

She's staring out the window, seemingly lost in thought. I think she's going to let my comment pass, but a few moments later, she breaks the silence. "You'd think so, wouldn't you? But I fear most of us lost touch with our humanity long ago. We've strayed too far into the darkness to even recognize the light should it find us."

I shrug, not knowing what to say. Her musings are almost lyrical, making me feel as if anything I say will be gauche by comparison. Which is absurd since I'm a published author who makes a good living with words. *If the subject were cock, you'd knock this out of the park. But this is like some Bob Dylan shit.* Then I open my mouth and say something that will probably offend the hell out of her. "If not for the bad people, how would we learn to appreciate the good ones?" *Dear God, her whole family is mafia. And now she thinks I'm a judgmental bible thumper. Aces.*

I regret what I've said almost immediately. Especially when she shifts until she's sitting in the corner with her face angled toward me. If I thought it was bad before, it's even worse now that she's entirely focused on me. Hell, she appears almost intrigued. I don't know her at all, but I sense that you don't want to be on this woman's radar. Unlike some who would get their way by pretending to be sweet and subservient to their family, she's the opposite. Marco and Rutger, heck, even Nic and Jake as well, have all commented on how scary she can be. But I have never really taken it seriously. Aren't all boys in awe of their mothers? I have to say, though, I get it. There's a backbone of steel under that cashmere sweater. Maybe it stands to reason that a man as powerful as Rutger would be attracted to and marry an alpha female. *No wonder Marco has an overload of testosterone.* "That's just it, Nina, there is truly no good or bad. Those terms shouldn't even exist. People are what others perceive them to be. A truly evil person may appear almost saintly if they act the part well. And the noblest of creatures can be deemed a monster if another knows where and how to plant the seeds of doubt."

Wow. Talk about a Negative Nancy. She is scary enough calm and composed. I certainly never want to see her lose her shit. "Um, yeah I guess that's one way to look at it," I concede.

"I can see why my son's infatuated with you," she muses. The random subject change has me struggling to keep up. "You back down when the conversation gets uncomfortable. A word of friendly advice for you, my dear. If that continues, he'll soon grow tired of it. My husband and my son are powerful men who are feared by many. They're used to being in charge and having others defer to their wishes. Don't get me wrong, there's nothing wrong with a man being a man, but without boundaries, they'll trample all over you without even noticing. It's something only a mafia wife could truly know."

Her show of concern doesn't fool me. This woman has no desire to see me with her son. I don't know what her end game is here, but it's not to help me out. Although, strangely enough, what she's said is the truth. And there's a big difference in me biting my tongue to keep the peace and being her son's doormat. *Screw it. She already hates me. Might as well go for broke.* "Mrs. Moretti, I can assure you that I am not now nor will I ever be Marco's punching bag—physically or verbally. A fact he's more than aware of, believe me. But you're right, I'm not a mafia. My last name might be Gavino, but that's on paper only. Whatever this is that I have with your son is between us. And although I appreciate your advice, I think I'll be fine. I may not be from your world, but I've been on the outskirts of it for many years as the stepdaughter of one of the city's most powerful men. Both he and his idiot son made damn sure I didn't suffer from weakness." *May have taken that a tad too far. Sunday brunch is probably off—forever.* "So anyway, I'm good."

She smiles, actually a genuine smile and not the fake ones I've received thus far. "I can see that," she murmurs approvingly. "And I'm glad." She turns away as if she's no longer interested in the conversation, which suits me fine. "That makes it so much easier."

"Pardon?" I ask, not sure I've heard her correctly, but she simply waves it off. Apparently, I'm not the only one here who does her thinking out loud. *At least it wasn't bitch. I think she's warming up to me.* I dart a quick glance in her direction and sag in relief when she pays me no attention. For a moment, I was terrified I did the same thing that she had.

The car swerves suddenly, and I'm pulled tightly against my seat belt. Angelica gives a squeak of alarm as well. "What's going on?" she calls out.

The driver who Jake had called Moose turns slightly, indicating he's heard her question. "It's nothing major, Mrs. Moretti. We passed a fender bender a while back, and they hadn't cleaned the glass up yet. I think we've got a flat tire. I'm looking for somewhere to pull over now. Shouldn't take long."

Angelica presses a hand against her chest and releases a breath. "Thank God, for a moment there I thought—"

"Shit. What happened?" My purse has flown from the seat during the commotion, and I lean down to pick up the contents. *Great, more time with Angelica. You're going to pay for this, Marco. I don't care if you have a freaky, hot body or not—Ouch, what was that?*

9

Marco

I can't help but think that Nina would laugh her ass off if she were here now. After all, meeting the crew in an underground bunker built under a coffee shop was kinda gangster. Of course, in the movies, it was usually a Chinese restaurant or something along those lines, but when the FBI decided to build a front so their field agents had a secure meeting location, it had seemed logical to pick a business where a person could reasonably be expected to patronage at all hours, instead of just the evenings. The owner of the place is one of ours and of course knows the score, but most of the employees don't. They're simply moved to other areas when we pass through the back to the cooler and the hidden panel behind it. "Cypher" is the code name for this long-running operation and stands for nothing. It's safer that way. Should your identity be compromised, all the bad guys would find is a bunch of random information that links nowhere.

My father is leaning against a wall drinking a cup of coffee when I walk in. Normally, several agents are here but not today. *Well, things just got interesting. The big man himself.* Hawk Malone is as big as they come and even though he and my father are friends, he's rarely seen in these parts. Instead, he's the force behind the scenes at Quantico in Virginia. He's always reminded me of Lee Jacks. Not in appearance—or his *undisputed* charisma—but in his abilities. He's rumored to have an IQ off the fucking charts, but men like him and Lee have something extra that sets them apart. It's that instinct, the intuition to pick one crumb from a pile of a thousand crumbs with no basis. Just a hunch—a feeling. These men are like a dog with a bone. Their determination and patience as they fixate on unexpected details—often resulting in a significant and unforeseen coup—is impressive. *Awe-inspiring.* That would, in theory, make Malone less than ideal to oversee the entire Southeastern division of the FBI, yet that's exactly what he does. He personally selects his SACs using the same process with which he solves a crime. Instinct. Intuitively knowing which agent is born to lead and who needs to follow.

This operation would have never been possible without a Moretti in the driver's seat. Because my father's parents moved away from North Carolina many years ago, he didn't grow up with his Moretti cousins. In fact, he was attending college in Upstate New York when Hawk Malone approached him. Draco Moretti came into power in the South almost overnight, and a much younger Malone was fascinated. He put feelers out, but Draco's men were fiercely loyal to him, so there was no weak link to be found. And Malone already sensed that the operation he randomly named "Cypher" would be both big and long-running. My father had turned him down countless times until my grandparents had been victims of a home invasion gone bad. My grandmother had died at the scene of a gunshot wound to the chest, and although my grandfather had lived an additional five years after, my father said he'd never been the same.

Ironically, that incident not only catapulted my father into the FBI but also opened the door for him with Draco. To his cousin, he was a man no longer content to play by the rules. He wanted to avenge his parents, and Draco was more than happy to offer his assistance. That's one thing outsiders never understood about the founder of the Moretti family. He could be completely without mercy when necessary. He was not only a leader, but he dominated—*ruled.* But he was also an odd sort of family man. Granted, his version of what that meant was distorted, but if you were loyal to him, that loyalty was rewarded. And that's exactly what he did for my father. He brought him slowly into the fold, making him privy to more of the operation in small increments. During this time, my father also met and fell in love with my mother at a party Draco hosted. Angelica King was the daughter of one of Draco's business associates. Reginald King laundered money through his chain of dry cleaners, for a fee of course. Although Victor Falco handled the majority of that for his best friend, it was always smart to spread your assets around, especially when you were talking astronomical amounts of money. It pleased Draco to have an official link with the Kings, so he gave his blessing on the marriage. A year later, I was born. My uncle's gift to me was an offshore account with one million dollars in it. *Guess he couldn't get to the store for diapers.*

By this time, Lee had long since proven to be Draco and Victor's greatest asset. They discovered a new world of possibilities just as lucrative and less risky. My father's own natural talents, along with Malone's guidance in the background, pushed my father forward quickly in the ranks until he was Draco's right-hand, his top lieutenant, and as such, he was privy to all.

The task force had started small. Malone, my father, and two other agents. Limiting the people involved meant less chance of leaks, and it had been the first of its kind. A long-term operation with not only a man who was an agent but also a relative to a mafia power. To most in law enforcement, the mission seemed simple. Infiltrate and dismantle. Take out the king and the rest would fall. But Malone had seen far-reaching gains. Greater longer-term benefits. Why be content with removing one faction from power if you could use it to take a dozen out? And while you were doing that, you also attained endless and valuable information on new power players and mafia transactions. For years, that's exactly what they'd done. The Morettis kept people out of Asheville and didn't give a fuck where the small-timers went afterward. And Malone would be there with a set of sealed indictments and snazzy handcuffs. It was his version of taking out the trash. The

Morettis were bagging that shit up for him and delivering it to his doorstep.

It was an unorthodox operation, at best, but with the extensive assets Malone was seizing on a regular basis, no one in power gave a good fuck. Just the opposite, in fact. They were elated. It was one of the biggest coups in FBI history, and it showed no signs of ending. Then Draco and Victor were murdered, and several things changed almost overnight. My father took over as head of the family, and I was old enough to realize there was more to him than met the eye. While he was busy riding the line between right and wrong, I was busy watching him. *Covertly.* It had taken a few months, but eventually, he caught on that he was being followed. But what finally gave *me* away was being caught breaking into his office—something I'd been doing on a regular basis for a while by that point. No one in the Moretti organization had a clue, but his twenty-one-year-old son had stumbled upon the truth. I didn't understand it all, of course, but I knew enough to be a problem, which presented a huge quandary. So I officially went away to "college." In reality, I was the new assistant to Malone and in a short time, his protégé.

It was a drastic step, one my father hadn't been happy about. And my mother even less so. By that time, she knew about my father's other life. There had been little choice really. She was simply too astute and had the home-field advantage. It would have required far too much time and energy to succeed in keeping a deception of that magnitude from her. Plus, a fully informed Angelica was a valuable person to have in your corner. She could also be counted on to contact Malone should something ever happen to my father.

I had grown up mafia, but being FBI was in my blood. I loved everything about it. And my excitement refueled Malone's. He became not only my mentor but also a second father to me. At the end of four years, it had been with both excitement and sadness that I returned home to assume my place in the family. Although, not in the way of my cousins. No, now I was the youngest member a task force that had grown to include both the DEA and the ATF. Unavoidable was the necessity to live a double life. I'd always been close to Nic and Jake, but I had to carefully filter my words to ensure I gave nothing away. In the beginning, it was difficult, and our interactions had felt stilted and awkward. Luckily, they blamed it on the fact that I'd been away at "yankee school" and needed to have the stick surgically removed from my ass. Thankfully, throughout the past twelve years, it has gotten easier in a way. I've lowered my guard more and more without fear of fucking up. Naturally, we all grew closer again, and slowly but surely, seeds of guilt continued to creep in.

I've developed a thicker skin, become a little jaded, *but* I still have my humanity. Meaning, feeling like a traitor still sucks ass. My only consolation is that we've given the family several layers of protection that weren't there before. None of the Morettis, nor Lee will ever go to jail for past actions. Nor will there be any legal consequences for any illegal activities they're ordered to do. They have complete immunity— if it's sanctioned by my father. If we're talking something big here, like an execution, then Malone must also sign it off. It's a complex situation where the lines between right and wrong have been so blurred at times, they were almost unrecognizable. We're not unlike a covert military op that goes into enemy territory and makes strategic kills; the ones you'll never read about in the paper but happen every day. There are operations so off-grid that even the president doesn't know they exist. We're not under that far, but we're deep. I haven't been in the same room with my father and Malone in ten years. That's why seeing him this morning is shocking. But worse than that, it's scary as fuck. If he's here, then there's a cataclysmic event unfolding, and one look at my father's face has me fearing it may already be too late to prevent the day of reckoning I've always known was coming.

10

Nina

When I roll over, the first thing I notice is how my tongue is stuck to the roof of my mouth. *Look out, world, some awesome morning breath coming through.* I flip onto my back as I struggle to push the sleep away. I feel as if I've been out for a year, yet my body is still unusually sluggish. Even though I don't recall it, I must have had a fitful night. God willing, I had a few sex dreams to make it worthwhile. I rub the backs of my hands over my grainy eyes a few times before the call of nature pushes me from the bed. It's either get up now or have my first adult bed-wetting episode. Minka would never let me live *that* down. Although Marco probably couldn't say much with his stomach issues. *Speaking of, where is he?* I automatically reach out to turn on the lamp—but it's not there. *What the?* I glance around the room in confusion, wondering if I'm dreaming. Surely, I must be. Everything is—wrong. *Boxed wine. Minka brought over another box of that cheap stuff she loves. Guess that explains why I slept in my clothes.*

The situation with my bladder is getting urgent. *Pee first, kill Minka later.* I get to my feet and walk stiffly toward the bathroom. My head is pounding. I don't recall drinking, but I obviously really tied one on last night. I reach the door and turn the handle, but it doesn't budge. *You've gotta be fucking kidding me.* All my good humor vanishes as I stand there with my ankles crossed. I figure I have about ten seconds to get to a toilet, so I let loose a volley of curses as I rush to the other door, intent on using the guest bathroom. Thankfully, that handle turns easily. Yet when I open it, there's no hallway. Instead, I'm in the bathroom. I know I haven't been at Marco's for long, but I'm quite sure his bathroom hasn't always looked like this. It's—fucking nasty. He had a cleaning woman, until recently, that is. How did things go downhill this badly in a week? *Heck, in eight hours.* I don't want to, but I have no choice. I hover over the toilet, careful not to make contact, and pee. Naturally, there's no toilet paper, not that I'd want to use it from this cesspool anyway. I shake off as well as I can, then walk to the sink to wash my hands. *Dear God, Marco. Even you're not hot enough to get away with being such a freaking pig.*

Then it's there. A realization akin to a lightning bolt. If I'm in the bathroom, then the bedroom door is locked. I hurriedly retrace my steps and try again because it's probably just stuck. But after a good five minutes of doing everything short of biting the damned handle off, I must face the facts: I'm locked in a room that I don't recognize, which is why I'm beginning to panic. Should I call out? Stay quiet? Before I make the decision, I move slowly around the room, really surveying my surroundings. Instead of Marco's floor-to-ceiling windows, these windows are small and up so high that I see nothing but the faint glow cast from external lighting. The bed is merely a mattress and box springs. There is no headboard, and God help me, no sheets. My skin crawls, and bile climbs up my throat as I stare at the stain-covered material I was sleeping on. Disgusting. The walls are a mixture of peeling wallpaper and chipped paint, and the floors appear to be plywood. I have a sinking feeling... am I in an abandoned house?

A normal person would be crying by now, and believe me, I want to. But I spent too many years with the Gavinos to lose sight of reality. *Scan the perimeter and look for threats.* Two of the most important things you can do in an unknown situation. *Oh... and don't lose your shit.* That one takes the top spot. I make my way slowly around the bedroom, checking for any clues as to where I am. By the third time around, I give up and search for anything that can be used as either a weapon or to help escape. Again, there's not much since the room is basically empty, but I do manage to pull a couple of loose nails out of the wood flooring and stick them under the side of the mattress for now.

As for avenues of escape, that one is tricky. With no windows in the bathroom and the ones in the bedroom being far from the ground, there's little hope that I'll be able to get out that way. Even with pushing the makeshift bed under them, they're still well out of reach. With limited options and even fewer resources, there's only one thing left available to me. And fuck it, even though I'm scared out of my mind, I give it everything I've got. I beat and pound on the bedroom door and toss in a couple of kicks to the wall for good measure. Having not seen any cameras, I also bring out my inner damsel in distress, hoping to lure whoever the hell has me into a sense of false security. Let them think I'm no threat so they might relax. Maybe get sloppy and give me an opening. That's all I need. One tiny sliver of opportunity and I'm gone. Either that... or I let them get close enough to plant one of those rusty nails in an eye or temple. It might not kill them, but they'll be in no shape to give chase. Most women grow up hearing when in danger, kick a man in the balls and you're home free. But that's simply not the case. First of all, they'll be expecting that. And most are born with that instinctive reflex to protect the family jewels. But what they're not expecting is a heel palm strike to the nose. The fragile cartilage there is easily broken, and although I have no first-hand experience, I've been told it hurts like a son of a bitch. Pretty much anywhere on the face is a winner. And a little-known fact, the ears are full of sensitive nerves. Pulling them will hurt *and* distract. My personal favorite is the throat. I hit Frankie Jr. there a few times through the years, and he flailed around like I stabbed him.

Unfortunately, I lose sight of all those objectives when the door suddenly opens because then I remember those last moments in the car. Flat tire. My purse flying from the seat and onto the floor. Leaning over to pick it up. *Pain.* "You can scream all you want, Nina. I can assure you there's no one around to hear. But I do find it rather annoying, so I'd appreciate it if you'd shut the fuck up."

"Oh my God," I hiss in dawning horror.

Dear God, I fall in love for the first time only to be taken out before we've even picked our china together.

To use one of Marco's favorite sayings—*fuck my life.*

Marco

Malone leaves his personal detail to secure the area while the three of us move deeper into the bunker. When the last steel door has locked behind us, he turns to pull me in for a hug. "How've you been, son?"

It's far from manly, but I feel a bit choked up. It's been so long since I've seen him in person, and until that moment, I had no idea how much I've truly missed him. We speak through encrypted forms of communication, but it's impersonal. "I'm good." I nod, noting he looks even more exhausted than usual. I doubt he's slept more than three hours at a time since he was an infant. He's both cursed and gifted to have a mind that never stops. And it's not usual drivel that keeps him awake. No, his mind is like a fucking heat-seeking missile. One that relentlessly searches for a target to lock on to and will not stop until it finds one. I used to envy him and wish I'd been born with the same abilities. But after working closely with him for years, that has changed. Like secondhand smoke exposure will shorten your lifespan, so will too much time around Malone. Human beings are not made to withstand the type of mental strain he places on himself. Maybe it's that way for all people with his level of intelligence—the hunger for knowledge and information that cannot be satisfied no matter how many times he feeds the beast inside. I glance from him to my father and back again. "Not to sound like a dick, but if you're here, I wish I were anywhere else."

My father smiles faintly while Malone laughs easily. He told me once that even though he preferred to work alone, he enjoyed the comic relief I brought to his life for the time I was there. *Pretty sure he liked the endless supply of McDonald's I brought with me as well.* My thoughts flash to Nina for an instant, remembering her love for that fucking McRib. Swear to God, I'll happily eat the calorie-laden thing with her if it means she'll never attempt to cook a single meal for me again. "Since when have you ever been concerned with my feelings, son?" he quips before motioning for us to take a seat at the conference table. Considering the bunker isn't often used, it's surprisingly clean and comfortable, and it's equipped with every type of technology we could need should we be forced to go to ground for any length of time. Now that we've exchanged the somewhat unnecessary small talk, Malone gets right to the point. "I've studied the police reports and other information available on both the Gavino murders and those of the Fosters. They were almost certainly committed by the same person. Weapon was a Glock G19." He opens a folder near his elbow and thumbs through some papers before tossing two onto the table. "Running the prints we pulled from the scenes took a fuck load of time. First off, the Gavinos weren't big on keeping the crime scene pure. The Foster family must have had a fair number of visitors since there were also multiple prints there." He leans back in his chair and crosses his legs at the ankles. "That one is puzzling. Killing someone so distantly linked to you is very random. No logical reason behind it at all. Not to mention, it points the finger at two people—one of whom should not have been at either scene."

I sit up straight and see my father do the same. We stare at that fucking folder like it holds the secrets to the universe. When he tosses a mugshot on top of the ballistics reports, I draw a harsh breath. My father reaches over and carefully picks up the paper, studying it thoughtfully. "We haven't been able to find a match on the first set, so we're still going through some local databases. Could be the person isn't in any databases. Makes identification tough, but not impossible. Hopefully, we'll get what we need from the one we do have. John Thomas Moretti. Booked ten years ago for an open container."

"Moose?" I murmur dazedly, still shocked by what we've discovered. Of course, I've considered it possible that one of our own family members was responsible, but Moose wasn't one who ever set off any type of alarm bells. Hell, he was just a low-level flunky. Mostly used for

running errands, maintaining our vehicles, and as a guard for mother
— "Fuck!" I jump to my feet, startling the other two. My father gives me
a questioning look as I run over to the desk in the corner and grab a
satellite phone from it. I quickly punch in a number and wait impatiently for it to be answered.

"Yeah?" I recognize Jake's voice on the other end. He won't recognize
this number since they change them about once a week, so I'm glad he
answers.

"Jake, it's me. Who's got eyes on my mother today?"

My father is on his feet now too as the implications of what I'm
saying hit him.

He's smart enough to understand when something's off and doesn't
waste my time with stupid questions. "Moose and Jimmy. Put Nina and
Angelica in the back of the Benz a couple of hours ago."

I swallow hard. *What the fuck is happening?* "Hang on a sec, man." I
write something on a piece of paper and hand it to my father. He takes
one of the other phones, and I hear him speaking in low tones before
disconnecting. The sound of him clicking that one button to end the
call seems so loud that I flinch. Of course, I realize it's the bleak expression on his face and not the phone at all—but in my mind, it might as
well have been a bomb. He gives one shake of his head. Nothing else.
He utters not another word, simply standing as if frozen in place. And
that is what terrifies me the most. My father, head of the most powerful
crime syndicate in the South, SAC of a legendary joint task force for the
FBI, and the most controlled person I've ever known, is afraid. And to
make matters worse, Malone appears just as grim. Malone points at the
phone I'm now clutching in my hand. Fuck, I forgot Jake was still holding. I clear my throat before asking, "Did anyone say where they were
heading?"

"The compound, brother."

I have no idea what, if anything, I say after that. I'm too busy shutting down the parts of me that'll distract me from my job. Before I turn
into the machine I'm trained to be when necessary, I allow one final
thought to flit through my mind: *the only two women I love may already
be gone, and fuck if I can listen to the logic that says this isn't my fault.*

11

Nina

"You bitch," I hiss in dawning horror.

"Now, now," she chides. "It's not polite to insult the mother of the man you're sleeping with. After all, what would my Marco think if he could hear you?"

Angelica and I have been locked in a stare off for what seems like an hour now but is probably more like five minutes. *What the hell is going on?* As much as I don't want to give her the satisfaction of me breaking first, this is getting me nowhere. Knowledge is the ultimate power. She has it, and I don't. I need to level that playing field if I have any hope of getting the fuck out of here. Heck, this could all be a misunderstanding. The car broke down, and we were forced to take shelter in the nearest crack house. She locked me in this charming, quaint bedroom for my own protection. After all, we're both women. Sisters before misters. Girl power. It might be easier to buy into that if she wasn't wearing a sinister smile. It's like a mix of bipolar June Cleaver and The Wicked Witch of the West. *I'll get you, my pretty...*

Pretend she's Minka, so always one-up. You got this. I yawn and glance around the room as if bored out of my mind. "You're one of those middle-aged empty nesters who has too much time on your hands, huh? Probably be easier if you had a career to fall back on. Instead, you got nowhere to go and all day to get there." I shrug my shoulder indifferently to add a little extra push, hoping it insults the hell out of her. Her cheek is twitching in a rather fascinating way. I wonder idly how she manages to keep the rest of her face smooth at the same time. *Too much Botox?* I don't verbalize that question—yet. I'll save that one for later.

"Middle-aged?" she parrots as if uncertain of the meaning. For a woman who obviously takes a lot of time and pride in her appearance, she probably doesn't know how to process the dig. *Well hell, bringing out the Botox now, after all.*

"You know, people over sixty-five." I know I've inflated the age, but I want this zinger to reach its target. "You're holding up pretty good there, Angie. You don't look a day over sixty. Heck, I bet when Marco and I have kids, they won't be able to believe you're their granny." I lower my voice, giving her a conspiratorial wink before I add, "Isn't Botox the best invention ever?" I point at her forehead, staring intently. "If not for the hairline wrinkles and the sagging eyelids, you'd look even younger. I bet a few more injections would take care of that, though. I read in *Cosmo* that geriatric women need the maximum amount every two months for maintenance instead of the usual three to four months." That last part might have been a bit of overkill. *Speaking of kill, my number may be up at any moment...* I force myself not to take a step backward as her partially frozen face fills with thunderclouds. Weirdly enough, she reminds me so much of Marco at that moment. *That's just... strange. Low blood sugar maybe?* To my knowledge, I haven't eaten today.

"I'll have you know, stupid girl, I'm nowhere near that age. Nor do I need Botox to look my best." She eyes me critically from top to bottom before adding, "Unlike you, I practice clean living. I don't eat processed junk, nor do I lay on my ass. I jog five miles a day and work with a personal trainer three times a week. From what I can see, none of those are part of your regime—"

"Is this where you lecture me about the youth of today?" I deliberately interrupt, knowing it will royally piss her off. *One homicidal Barbie, coming right up.* "How back in your day, you walked ten miles through the snow with no shoes to get to your one-room school. No electricity or television." I bring my hand up, making a flapping motion. I'm used to exchanging barbs with Minka, so it's entirely too easy for me to toss way too many insults in a short amount of time. *The goal here is information, not assassination.*

She surprises me, though, by shaking it off. In fact, I wonder if she blanked out during my entire rant, which is rather disappointing since it was some of my better stuff. "You have no children, Nina, so I realize this may be hard for you to grasp, but when you become a mother, there's a shift inside you. Oh, you're still the same person, but you have a vulnerability that you will never overcome. As much as you may have loved another, it doesn't compare to the unconditional love you have for the child you carry within you for nine months. There's a bond there—a link that only grows stronger. You read books or magazines that say eventually they'll grow up, leave home, and make their own way in the world. Those articles lead you to believe at that point, you simply wash your hands of them and move on. You no longer worry, nor miss them when they're gone. But that's not the case. I've found the opposite to be true. When Marco was a child, I had the usual worries. Him falling off his bike, out of a tree, or being abducted by a rival family." *For a moment, that had been almost normal.*

She pauses, giving me an expectant look. I've been bad cop the past few times, so I decide to try out the good one. Might as well keep her off balance. *Thinking the whacko ship has already sailed there.* "Um, I'm sure all parents have been there. My mom probably worried about the same things. But you must be proud of the way he turned out. He's a respected mafia guy. At the top of the food chain. What else could you possibly want for him?" *Okay, so there was a slight amount of sarcasm, but I'm not a saint.*

She stares off into the distance as if intently pondering my question. *Either that or deciding in which manner to kill me.* "For starters, I would prefer he find a much better class of women to spend time with. Your last name may be Gavino, but you're an outsider." *And damn proud of it, Granny.* I'm so busy tossing around insults in my head, that I almost miss her next words. "But most importantly, I wish he'd never followed in his father's footsteps and joined the FBI. Now, not only is my husband a traitor to the family but also my son."

I got nothing. Total blank. Points for creativity, girlfriend. "Yeah, I feel your pain," I say in a voice oozing with sympathy. "It always chapped my ass when Franklin pretended he was Santa. Come on, he didn't even have a beard. And using Frankie Jr. as his elf? Not only scary but kinda disturbing as well." *I've gotta remember to tell Minka this one. Frankie Jr. an elf. Priceless.*

A look of something akin to approval flashes across her face. *It's probably just gas.* "I wasn't expecting you to believe me immediately, Nina, but I will say, I admire your calm manner, even in difficult circumstances. I see a lot of your mother in you. She was an outsider too, but always so quick with a joke. In another world, I believe that we all could have been friends."

I have no idea if she's tossing the friend card out there for my mother or me, but I'm pretty sure my mother thought she was a raging bitch as well. "Well, thanks for that," I say grandly. "It's always cool to get the seal of approval from your man's mommy. I'll check that one off the list." *I'm rather impressed with myself that I'm still wisecracking. I owe you BIG, Minka. If not for years of insane conversations with my best friend, this wouldn't be possible.* When she turns to pick up something, I notice what appears to be her purse against the wall. I find it hard to believe even a woman as vain as Angelica would stop at this point to check her makeup. Maybe I've pushed too far and hit her limit. Those pants are probably too tight for a gun, so no doubt it's in her bag. But instead of the glint of metal, it's more like a stack of papers. Oh, great. She's probably going to offer me a million bucks to stop banging her son. Got her lawyer to draw of a contract for me to sign. *Ms. Gavino agrees to no longer ask Mr. Moretti to slap her ass or put anything else in said orifice—*

I'm rather enjoying my brief naughty flashback when she clears her throat. "As I was saying, I didn't expect you to believe me immediately, so I took the liberty of bringing some... visuals you might find of interest." She shoots me a look full of concern, and that has the hairs on the back of my neck standing at attention. "I'll warn you, dear, these are a bit... graphic in nature, and you may find them upsetting." I half-expect an offer to hold my hand, but thankfully, it doesn't come.

I'm nervous, but thanks to years of practice, my hand is steady when I thrust it out. "Yeah, yeah, thanks for the concern. Let's see what you got, *Angie*." She squints at me with derision and scorn, which is not a good look and probably messing with her Botox. She hates my short-ened version of her name, but she doesn't comment. *I think she liked me calling her bitch better. At least it's more accurate.* I'm not sure what I was expecting when I pull the stack from her hand, but seeing my stepfa-ther lying on his back with his eyes open wasn't on the list. At first, I'm puzzled. Then I see it—the hole in his forehead. Of course, Marco told me how he died, but shouldn't there be more damage? Where's the blood? I swallow hard, then look at the next one. *Frankie Jr.* He's posi-tioned eerily like his father. Yet there is no bullet hole. I know why a moment later when the next page shows a picture of the back of what I presume is his head—only there's a chunk missing. *Utterly horrifying.* I've never been more grateful to have watched the oftentimes gory tele-vision show, *Bones*. Otherwise, these images would have me throwing up at the very least. *Just like on television. Make-believe. Not real, not real.*

There's no way to control it now, my body is trembling, and I hate this woman in front of me for it. "Read the bottom of the page, Nina," she murmurs.

"*Targets successfully terminated. Cypher ID: MM.*" I glare at her, wanting to wrap my hands around her throat. "This proves nothing. Big deal, you got your hands on some autopsy reports. Even I could do that."

"Tsk, tsk, you're smarter than this, Nina. Use your head and think. Why would I bother telling you any of this if it were not true?"

"Because you're a sadistic old lady," I hiss. Strangely enough, the verbal sparring centers me again, and the shaking begins to subside. *Shift your focus. Push everything else aside.*

The dig at her age doesn't appear to bother her this time, though. Instead, she lifts her shoulders in a *whatever* gesture before looping the straps of her purse over her shoulder. "I'm sure you could use some alone time to process what you've learned." She glances at her watch, all business now. "I have important business to attend to, and I've already waited far too long."

"Going to boil someone's bunny or kill their cat?" I sneer in disgust. I really, really despise her.

"Oh no." She smiles brightly. "I'm going to call my husband and let him rescue me from this horrible situation. I'm in shock, so it's going to take some time to recover." That part is said in a voice so full of grief and terror that even I'm riveted. *How long has she... despised her husband to be able to lie so convincingly?* "And the guilt I'll feel as the sole survivor. Losing not only my husband but you as well. We formed such a bond during this horrid abduction. It'll be hard, but I'll be strong for my son."

"You're certifiable," I mutter.

She appears to almost pity me for a moment. "You cannot truly judge another until you've walked in their shoes, my dear. I sacrificed my entire life to push Rutger to the top. Do you think a man like Draco didn't exact a price for every good deed? It wasn't so tough. He was a handsome man and amazing in bed. I enabled Rutger's way up the ladder on my back, and Draco took the final step by dying." She's almost screaming by this point, which shows me more than her words how unhinged she's becoming. "We could have had it all, but even then, he couldn't turn his back on the fucking FBI." Then—just like flipping a switch—calm Angelica is back. "It's only fitting he should be killed in the line of duty. And with him gone, Marco will be free of his influence, and he'll do what I advise him to do. He's always listened to his mother. Unfortunately, my hands were tied when he joined the FBI, but after Rutger's death, he'll turn to me and the *family* for comfort and support. From there, all will fall into place." She turns up her nose before adding, "I'll help him recover from your death at the hands of that traitor Moose as well." She sounds like a demented soccer mom as she adds, "That's what good mothers do."

And finally, it hits me like a punch to the gut. I was dead from the first moment I crossed paths with Marco. Because Angelica has a plan for him, and she won't allow anything to get in the way of it. Before I can respond to the information dump she's heaped at my feet, she leaves the room. The pictures of Franklin and Frankie Jr. slip from my nerveless fingers to the floor, and I slump to my knees, mere inches away from them. "Cypher," I whisper. *Where have I heard that name before?* "Cypher." It's an elusive puzzle piece that hovers just out of my reach. *Cypher.* Then I have it.

A seemingly random moment in time that I discounted because it had meant nothing. *It can't be a coincidence.* I go down completely then, making full contact with the hardwood as I curl into a fetal position. Dimly, I understand this is the worst time possible to have a break-down, but when you discover something this big, then even the toughest of women need a time-out, and whether it's advisable or not, my body has taken one. Before I completely shut down, I shake my head in anger and confusion. If what Angelica Moretti said is true, the man I love isn't simply a mafia thug. He's a liar. A well-trained killer. Someone I should despise.

So how can part of me hate Marco while the other part is desperate for him?

Marco

A dozen agents, my father, Malone, and I are staring at three different screens. One shows the GPS coordinates of my mother's car, the second is the location of Nina's shoes. While she showered one evening, I placed trackers in the soles of every pair when I discovered she was sneaking out. And the last is a satellite image of the area. The GPS shows Nina close to the vehicle, which is a relief in a way. At least we won't be forced to split our manpower in two directions. But it makes me nervous as well that there's been no movement from her dot since we've been monitoring it. Both my father and I were ready to take off as soon as we got a hit on the location, but Malone stopped us by pointing out that we would be putting the women in danger by going off half-cocked. There has been no signal from my mother, Moose, or Nina's phone, so clearly, they've been shut down. "All right, the initial scouts are nearing the area now, so let's move out. By the time we reach them, they should have the perimeter secure."

We're moving out of the bunker in single file when his two-way radio beeps. "Ghost reports three. Two females, one male. Advise your men there's a friendly in the area."

"Who in the fuck is Ghost?" I ask in confusion. Naturally, most operatives have code names for security, but I don't recognize the voice on the radio. Nor should we have a man there ahead of our scouts.

We're at the last door before exiting into the coffee shop when Malone stops and releases a deep breath of resignation. "Ghost's an undercover operative from the ATF and has been embedded for about ten years."

My father is ticked and probably a little hurt. He considers Malone not only his boss, but a friend, and to have something like this withheld is a slap in the face. "There's a third, and I was never informed? You've had someone watching over us? If you don't trust me, Hawk—"

"Jesus, Rutger," Malone utters. "This has nothing to do with trust. This agent has a completely different objective. There is no snooping around the Morettis. You know me better than that. If I didn't trust you, then you wouldn't fucking be here. Either of you."

"Who the hell is it?" my father asks. Malone looks away, clearly not wanting to reveal what he knows. My father looks poised to strike when his phone rings. We rarely have a signal on our regular phone deep within the bunker, but it normally returns when we're closer to the entrance. "Christ," he hisses as he connects the call. "Rutger." A look of pure shock crosses his face when he utters, "Angel?" My pulse leaps as he calls out the nickname he's always had for my mother. He listens intently, firing off a series of questions about the location and situation. I know it sucks, but we're trained to push emotions aside and zero in on the facts. Those are what save lives. Hysteria weakens. "Yes, I'm aware that Moose is involved." There are a few more nods from him before he says, "Nina? I see... keep pressure on the wound. We're... Angel? Angelica!"

He lowers the phone slowly before looking at me. "Angelica and Nina staged an attack on Moose. While he was fighting with Nina, the gun he was holding went off, and she took a round to the chest. Angelica hit him in the head with a fucking toilet cover. He dropped the gun, and she grabbed it and put a round in him. Says he's dead, but Nina's still alive. Thinks she's going into shock from the blood loss." Malone is on his radio calling for a medevac before I can even process what we've learned. My father moves to stand directly in front of me, putting a hand on each of my shoulders. "Focus, Marco. Do the job. Leave the rest." There's sorrow in his eyes that tells me he's not really living what he's preaching at this point, but he's right. If I fall apart, she has no chance. I have one final thought before I go carefully blank. *Don't you dare die on me, Belle.*

12

Nina

I expected Angelica back by now, but so far there's been nothing. I get to my feet, shaking my self-pity and doubts aside. *I will not give you the pleasure of killing me, bitch.* I look around the room once again, searching for anything that'll get me out of here. *The nails.* After pulling them from their hiding place under the mattress, I stick one in my pocket and approach the door. It's an old lock, and those are usually the easiest to pick. Why did I waste precious time with the whole pity-party thing when I could be escaping? I'm even more exasperated when I have the damn thing unlocked in all of two minutes. *Not my proudest moment. No way am I telling Minka that part.* It creaks so loudly when I open it that I expect to see Angelica at any moment. *Come to think of it, where are the damn guards?* I hesitantly slip my head out into the hallway. It's dim and musky smelling but deserted. I slide my back against the wall, trying not to think of what I'm brushing past, and go in the direction I hope leads me to an exit. I keep waiting for something, anything to startle me, but I literally walk straight up to and out the back door without a hitch. *This is all wrong.* Where in the hell is Angelica? Even Marco will be impressed if I make it out of this alive. *What if I never see him again? Why do I even care? He's a liar and God knows what else. Yet... stop it. Shelter first, questions and heartbreak later.*

I'm standing at the bottom of the steps choosing my direction when an unmistakable click sounds behind me. "Really, dear, I didn't think you'd ever take some initiative. A five-year-old could have picked that lock. What took you so long? The cavalry is on the way, so I need to wrap this up."

My brain is urging me to run, but at this distance, she'll easily hit me. No, my only option is to catch her off guard and buy a few extra seconds. That's all I'll need. So I turn slowly to see Angelica standing near the top step, holding a gun. The sound I heard had been her chambering a round. It seems insane that she would not have already loaded the gun, but who am I to judge? *This lady is seriously batshit crazy.* I open my mouth to say something that will likely get me killed, but in the end, that isn't necessary.

The blast knocks me off my feet. I've barely processed that when my chest is on fire. I clumsily bring a hand up, trying to push aside whatever's crushing me. My vision dims, and my reality is distorted. Fragments of sound and motion flit around me, but it's as if I'm watching from a great distance. *It's a dream, it must be.* How else would Minka be standing over me with her gun drawn as she screams my name?

Why is it so cold?

Why is everything... so dark?

Marco

Our radios are going wild as we arrive at the old farmhouse. "Stand down, stand down! Friendly fire. I repeat, stand down. Do not fire. Agent is securing the scene." Another beep sounds. "Ghost, advise. Has the threat been eliminated?"

We all wait with bated breath. I hope to God Moose is dead, but I'll be much happier if I put him down myself. *Belle, hold on.* "Threat eliminated, but get the fucking medevac here now, asshole. Gunshot wound to the motherfucking chest." The last part comes out as more of a sob than a shout, which is somehow even more terrifying.

"Ghost is a woman?" my father asks absently as we run toward the house. *I could give a fuck if she's a woman or the pope at this point. My Belle.*

Malone mutters something I can't make out. Another agent points us toward the back, and I vaguely hear the medevac landing in a nearby field, but all that is just background noise. But then I see something that brings me out of my haze and crashes me into a reality I could have never imagined. A blonde is huddled over something on the ground, and she's cursing and saying shit that makes no sense. "You remember when you broke my Wonder Woman snow globe, and I sewed all your shirt sleeves up? Well, I'll do much worse if you don't get your shit together. I'll tell Marco you have Google alerts set up on him. And that you have a picture of him as your iPad background." Then the ranting stops, and my blood runs cold as a loud keening fills the air. "I swear to God, Nina Gavino, if you leave me, I'll never forgive you. I can't live in a world that you're not a part of. You and me forever, we promised each other. We promised."

Minka? What? Why is she here? My mind is slow to comprehend what my eyes are telling me. *Ghost is a woman? A woman. Minka?* My bewilderment is pushed aside as we all stand frozen, transfixed by her all-consuming grief. I've never loved like this before—it's been limited to family—until Nina. But I've never witnessed the type of bond that would bring this level of despair. I'm not even sure I'm capable of that depth of feeling—or so I thought. Three things show me that not only can I reach that level, I can surpass it: seeing Minka being physically lifted from her protective crouch over her best friend's body is bad; Nina lying utterly still and deathly pale with a crimson bloom covering her chest has me shaking in reaction; and finally, hearing my father's shout of alarm and numbly turning to see him clutching my mother against his chest as he screams her name.

Malone is before me now. His lips are moving, yet I hear nothing but a buzzing in my ear. My earlier thoughts are confirmed in the most horrifying fashion imaginable.

This is a cataclysmic event unfolding. Focus. Do the job. From out of nowhere, one thought rises above the wreckage around me, and my mouth drops open incredulously. "You knew."

He doesn't reply, but the look on his face tells me all I need to know. "Focus," he says softly.

I see Nina being loaded onto a stretcher, and there's no longer an internal debate. "Vitals are stable for the moment. Let's get her out of here." The team working on my mother gives a sign I've seen before. *Dead at the scene.*

My father looks shell-shocked, but he would be the first to tell me to go with the woman I love. And that's exactly what I do. "Fuck the job," I toss out as I push past Malone and join Minka and the emergency team. I'll have my answers later, but right now, there is only the woman on the stretcher fighting for her every breath. The beautiful spitfire who once saved my life. And I will call in every marker owed to me to save hers.

13

Marco

"You're beginning to stink." Minka wrinkles her nose from a nearby chair before fanning her face. We've both been keeping vigil at Nina's bedside since she was rushed in two days ago, and it's been touch and go since then. She was taken straight into surgery where they were able to remove the bullet. However, a lung had been punctured along with a host of other issues that I tried not to even think about. At the last update, her doctor assured us that she was stable and holding her own, but she was nowhere near out of the woods yet. The fact she was covered with tubes, wires, and monitors certainly gave truth to that fact. If I had to pick one that scared me the most, it was the damn tube in her mouth. It makes me feel as if she would die instantly if it were removed. Minka said something similar the first time we saw her.

Unfortunately, our visiting time is limited since she's in ICU. But we've swayed a few sympathetic nurses who allow us a little extra when possible. I rub my eyes, trying to remember when I last slept. *Days?* "Let's agree not to comment on each other's hygiene. Because you're not faring much better."

She smiles faintly before getting to her feet and approaching the bed. "I was jealous of you, still am. When you puked your way into her life, she changed."

Her back is to me, and for a moment, I think she's talking to Nina. Then she turns, and I realize this is about me. "She's had a few boyfriends over the years—we both have. But there was never anything serious. We have been each other's significant others since the day we met." A half-smile curves her lips before she adds, "And not in a gay way. It's hard to describe. We're like the missing piece the other needs to be whole. Before Nina, I never had anyone close to me. My dad worked all the time, and I never even knew my mother. Plus, when you're in 'the family,' being friends with outsiders doesn't really work. I didn't click with the few who were my age within our circle, so I spent most of my time alone. I told myself that's the way I wanted it. That it was my choice." She stares off into the distance for so long I think she's finished, which is strangely disappointing because I'm enjoying hearing the backstory of how these two formed such a bond. "Then one day, she was there. Franklin had a new wife, and everyone was invited over to welcome her. There stood this girl who no one was paying any attention to except me and my dipshit cousin, Frankie. I didn't approach her right away. But I tailed her for the rest of the evening and caught Frankie harassing her. I drove my knee in his balls, and the rest is history. Some people form friendships over drinks or common interests, but ours was over mutual hate for Frankie."

"Yet you never told her you were in the ATF." Naturally, I, better than anyone, understood that she wasn't at liberty to. But still, these two didn't appear to keep secrets from each other—much less something of that magnitude. "How'd that come to pass, anyway?" Neither of us has mentioned the surprise revelation until now because our sole focus has been Nina. Other than medical personnel, I haven't seen anyone but Minka since we've been here. My father hasn't reached out to me, nor I to him. Minka has given me a brief version of what transpired as she knows it, but I've cut her off halfway through. I can't—not now. My mind is not ready to deal with, nor accept, the reality she has begun to describe. And my father is much like me in the respect that he will want to be alone for now. All else can wait.

It's too fucked up.

My mother committed the worst type of crime—betrayal.

"In much the same manner that it did for you probably. I was recruited by the ATF. Approached on a weekend trip to New York. I was in a bad place then. Angry with the world and feeling so damn helpless because I couldn't do anything about it. Nina and I had planned a girls' weekend away. My father had agreed to a big shopping spree in New York, and I was beyond excited. Then Nina ended up with bronchitis a few days before we were supposed to leave. I told her we'd wait and go in a few weeks, but she wouldn't hear of it. She knew I needed the time away, and I've never been able to tell her no. Of course, I had a low-level flunky clone as a guard, but he was lazy and easy to ditch when I wanted to. I suspect he was enjoying the area whores, so he certainly wasn't complaining, nor telling my daddy when I gave him the slip. So it was easy for someone to approach me in a coffee shop there. I told the guy to fuck off, but something made me keep his card." She reaches down and gently brushes a hair from Nina's forehead as she begins speaking again. "Months passed, and I couldn't get it out of my head. I finally called the number and arranged another meeting, closer to home. What finally made me agree was the promise of immunity for my father and if needed, Nina. As well as protection for them in an emergency."

"How were you trained?" I ask, intrigued despite myself. Other than my father, I have never been able to talk about my other life with anyone, and it feels surprisingly good.

"The old college excuse." She laughs. "Same for you?"

"Yeah." I smile. "But I went away for college, technically. How did you pull it off?"

"Stayed in North Carolina, but it was all a front anyway. Of course, on paper, I was there every day. It would have passed scrutiny by most anyone. But my actual education was held in an older building on campus that was no longer used. After I graduated, I went to work. Only, like you, my job was going home and appearing normal. Which, in my case, was being the hellion daughter of Ray Gavino. Bad attitude and an even worse temper. Since the Gavinos dealt in arms more than

the Morettis, that was my focus. I supplied the ATF with as much information as I could. And when we pushed the competition out, the ATF
picked them up after a reasonable amount of time passed."

"Sounds like our operations were very similar," I marvel, knowing
that Malone must be behind this. Truthfully, I don't really know how I
feel about it.

The door opens, and we both go on instant alert. Luckily, most
would put it down to life within the mafia and not federal agents. Ida,
the night nurse, walks in, giving us both a bright smile. "Hey, you two. I
heard our girl's doing much better." Minka steps back while the nurse
checks the monitors. "You're way past visiting hours, and my supervisor
is here tonight, so be good and leave peacefully so I won't get in trouble." She winks as she adds the last part, and we have no choice but to
reluctantly agree.

Minka kisses Nina on the cheek and murmurs something in her ear
that I can't hear. Then I lean over to do the same. "I'll eat all the lasagna
you want. Just come back to me, Nina." I pause for a moment, then
unable to hold the words in any longer, I add, "I love you." *You should be
awake to hear me say that, Belle. If not for my mother—*

Don't. Can't go there.

I press one last kiss on her temple and follow Minka out. I come to
an abrupt stop when I see Malone coming down the hallway toward us.

He exchanges a few words with Minka before turning to eye me
warily. "Marco, can we talk? I can wait if you need to get back to Nina."

I push my hands into my pockets, feeling strangely like a kid. I'm
afraid to hear the truths I'm not ready to acknowledge. When Minka
was telling me her version, I'd been able to push it aside and pretend
she didn't know what she was talking about because she's confused by
her grief. But Malone deals in facts. And there's no escape from those. I
feel a hand on my back and glance over at Minka in surprise. She leans
in closer, murmuring, "You can't get past it until you face it. Do it for
Nina." *Fuck. I can't argue with that.* "I'm going to visit my father. He's
almost recovered now, but he'll be on crutches for another few weeks. I
swear I've never heard a grown man act like such a baby." I was glad to
hear that Ray was going to be okay after the attack on him that left his

guard dead. Regardless of their relationship, I don't think Minka could have handled losing him or Nina.

Without another word, I follow Malone wordlessly to the parking lot and climb into the passenger seat of a nondescript sedan. Instead of starting the engine, we simply sit there in silence. Finally, he says, "Do you want the details? I know you've pieced most of it together by now, but I'll fill in the blanks if you're ready for it. Up to you, son."

I take a deep breath and nod. "Do it."

"Moose was still alive when we searched the house. He had a gunshot wound to the abdomen and one to the right shoulder. When he saw your father, he knew it was over. He told him that Angelica had approached him with the story that Rutger was physically abusive. How she feared for not only her life but yours as well. She also lured him in with a bit of a... romantic element, and he thought he was essentially saving his soul mate from peril. She came up with the scheme of pitting the Gavinos against the Morettis after the hit on Franklin and his son. She figured it would all tie in nicely. Eventually, she planned to kill Rutger and figured it could be easily blamed on the Gavinos as retaliation for Franklin."

I put a hand to my temple, massaging the pressure point as I attempt to sift through what he's telling me and make sense of it all. "But what about the car bomb? Did she intend to kill me as well, her own fucking son?" *Had I ever known the woman who raised me? Who claimed to love my father and me more than anyone? Or pretended to. Was any of it real, or had our entire life as a family been a lie?* I only thought I understood how Tony must have felt at his uncle's betrayal. Now I know that wasn't the case. The utter pain, disbelief, and anguish. The rage. *I had no fucking clue—until now.*

Malone shakes his head, before saying, "According to Moose, the bomb was a massive fuckup. It was on a timer to explode inside your garage with you nowhere around. You activated it when you fired the ignition. Otherwise, it would have gone off itself on the backup timer. Since you rarely drove yourself, they had no clue you'd suddenly decide to drive that night you went to Nina. It was planted to keep attention focused to the Gavinos."

Then I remember something else that never made sense to me. "What about the Fosters? What possible reason could there have been to take them out?"

"Wrong place, wrong time. Apparently, your mother dropped by to visit you at some point while Langdon was hiding at your place. Moose was her guard that day, and they took advantage of your absence to discuss their operation. When she got word that you'd had a stowaway, she panicked, thinking they might have been overheard. She couldn't get to Langdon since he was always with Jake, but she eliminated his family on the outside chance he'd talked to them about it. She intended to get to the boy, but when nothing was ever mentioned, she let it slide." *Who is this woman? I have no fucking clue how I missed any of these signs.*

I sag back against the seat and ask the one question that puzzles me the most. "Why? What could possibly have made her do this? She loved my father; I know that wasn't all an act." *Fuck, please don't let everything have been a lie. I need something to hold on to. One thing that was real.*

"I believe that to be true," he says. "But she loved being mafia more. A lot of the rest is just speculation without her to verify it. Naturally, Moose's version is distorted by feelings and what she wanted him to believe. I gather the goal was to get rid of your father and put you in power. She figured you'd be disillusioned with the FBI and ready to take your place as the rightful head of the family. And that's what she always wanted. To be an ultimate power."

"And Nina wasn't part of that picture, was she?"

"No, she wasn't. She belongs to neither side, and that's not what Angelica wanted for her only son. She probably figured that should Nina remain, she would weaken her hold on you." *Her hold on me? Had I ever felt that she had a hold on me? No. Never.* Have I missed signs all along that my mother thought I was easily converted to her way of thinking? And had Malone seen that?

"Did you know? Something brought you here. I knew it that day in the bunker."

He taps his fingers on the wheel for a moment in a way that sounds like nails on a chalkboard. "I told you we pulled two sets of prints that were at both the Foster's and Gavino's. There was no match in the databases for the second set, but there was an oddity. They were small, which indicated they belonged to either a woman or a child. I'm sure there are men out there with hands that size, but it bothered me. It triggered *that* feeling. The one that I get when—"

"I remember well how those hunches consume you. So you thought if you got closer to the action, you might be able to unravel the mystery."

"Exactly," he says. "But sadly, it escalated so quickly it was over almost before it started. For as many good outcomes as we have, far too many also go the other way. I've become jaded to them over the years. But this one, it's going to haunt me for a long time."

Thinking we're both in need of a subject change, I ask him, "Where is Moose now? And what of Jimmy? He was also part of the detail?"

"We found Jimmy's body about a mile from the house. Moose pretended to lose control of the car, claiming a flat tire. During the confusion, your mother shot Nina up with a strong enough sedative to knock her out, and Moose sent Jimmy to check the door. While he was doing that, Moose shot him in the back of the head."

"Fuck."

"Rutger terminated Moose after we interrogated him. He knew far too much; he could not be allowed to live, even in a maximum security prison."

"How's he doing?" I ask softly, feeling like a shitty son and man for not reaching out to him before now. *Coward. Didn't want it to be real.*

"Marco, your father made a decision that day. I advised against it, but in the end, it was his call. And likely the only opportunity he would have for a while." He has my full attention again now. My mind whirling with the implications. "The official statement is Moose shot your father, then Angelica killed Moose and finally herself."

Stunned.

When I think nothing else can touch me, the world is shaken around me once more. "They . . . the family won't believe that. There needs to be proof."

He appears almost insulted for a moment. "Marco, this is the FBI. The proof has already been taken care of. As far as the family is concerned, that's exactly the way it happened. They are aware that Nina was involved but managed to get away. Your call to Jake tipped them off that something was wrong. Nic also knows that Minka escaped the compound, and she told him that she traced Nina's phone before it had been turned off. We've tied up all the loose ends in the past two days. The only thing left is for you to assume your place as the head of the family."

"You must be fucking kidding me," I say in astonishment. "Just like that? Back to taking out the trash for you."

He rolls his eyes. Not something I saw him often do through the years. "If you'd give me a moment before jumping to conclusions, I'll explain." I wave my hand grandly, waiting to hear what he could believe would make any difference to me. "It's your choice if you want to continue with the Bureau. I promised you that in the beginning, and it still holds true. But, outside of that, you essentially run a business that employs many of your family. It also keeps a lot of assholes out of the city. If you walk now, someone else assumes control, and believe me, there isn't an active Moretti left that can hold and wield that type of power. You'd ultimately destabilize the area in more ways than one. Even if you can protect yourself, you leave a lot of others in a very vulnerable position—including Nina. If you're smart, you'll take the reins, steer the company in the manner that Lee Jacks has his, and slowly take the holdings as close legal as possible. Your father has already solidly paved the way for just that."

"And exactly where is my father now that he's *deceased*?" My feelings toward my parents are near mind-fuck levels right now. Of course, I know my father is innocent and was even more a victim than I am. Hell, he's the real victim in all this. Yet people are rarely rational when faced with tragedy and betrayal, and I'm no different. A part of me resents him for joining the FBI and bringing this fallout to our door, and a part of me feels the devastation and anguish that must be tearing him to pieces. *He loved her so much. His heart must be broken for more than one reason.* In a perfect world, and a normal family, we'd be together, dealing with our grief and finding a way to heal. But we're not your typical family, and we've always handled things differently. In this instance, my father does not want to see me, nor I him. For as much as we love each other, we must process our grief separately. At some point in the future, when the wound is not so raw and the horror so fresh, we'll see each other again, but until then, we survive. We move forward and attempt to pick up the tattered pieces of our lives—if that's even possible.

"He's off the grid for the foreseeable future. When you're ready, I'll point you in that direction. I'll supply updates periodically for peace of mind if you'd like."

"Thanks." I nod absently. "How can you be sure that no one in the family has gotten wind of your presence here? It would have been hard to hide your guys skulking around."

He smiles faintly. "We don't skulk. And our local police contact handled all associations with the family. They've met him before, so there was no reason to suspect anyone else was involved. Since Nina was injured on the scene, your father called 9-1-1 for her, hence the notification of the police. This isn't our first rodeo, son."

Cocky bastard. "What of Minka? I assume you recruited her?"

"You know I cannot discuss another agent with you, especially one from another entity altogether. And her future is between her and the ATF. I'm quite certain that she's put similar stipulations in place, so ultimately, it'll be up to her."

We talk for a few more minutes before he darts a glance at his watch. "I'm sorry, son, but I've got to go. I have a plane to catch in less than an hour." I have my hand on the door handle when he adds, "Think about what I've said. Your family will be looking at you for answers and reassurance. Give them the leader they need—at least for now. The rest can wait. Oh, and I'd touch base with Nic and Jake. They're getting antsy. They know Nina was admitted to the hospital, but she's under an alias, and unless you've missed it, she's the only one on the fourth floor. No one other than staff and you two have been allowed up."

I look at my mentor one more time saying softly, "Thanks for everything. I'll think about what you've said and let you know my decision. And tell my father I'll be in touch when the time is right." I *want* to console him. I want to grieve with him as his loss is great. Fuck, how were we both so blind? But not yet. *And he'd hate to see pity or sympathy from me.* Malone inclines his head, and I get out of the car and stand there until his taillights disappear in the distance.

I'm a few feet away from the entrance to the hospital when a vehicle pulls in, blocking my path. I instantly go into full alert until I recognize the black Escalade and Nic behind the wheel. He rolls down the window, saying simply, "Get in." I'm so fucking exhausted by this point, I don't bother to argue. "Your place?" he asks, but I simply shake my head. I'm not sure I can ever go back there again. Too many memories.

He doesn't say anything further, and I lay my head wearily against the glass of the passenger window as we move through the city streets. We arrive at his place about fifteen minutes later, and he points to the direction of the guestroom. It's then I realize how much I've missed him. And how badly I need some normalcy. I give him a brief hug, and he returns it silently, then I go straight to the bed in the other room and pass out.

Light is spilling into the room when I wake up. I panic, afraid that something may have changed with Nina, but when I text Minka, she assures that she's still stable. *Thank fuck. I can't lose her now. Not after all this.* I have no idea how long I've been out, but I feel more human. Nic has left a change of clothes out for me, and I take a quick shower and dress. Nic is sitting on the sofa flipping channels when I walk in, and he gives me a cursory once-over. "You look a little less like shit now," he quips.

I grin faintly, dropping down next to him. "Thanks for this," I say, meaning more than just the sleep and clothes.

For always having my back.

For knowing when to stay away.

For knowing when I need you.

For so fucking much more than I can say...

"Sorry about everything, brother. I just—fuck, I don't know what else to say."

"That makes two of us," I say wearily. "I'm not ready to deal yet. May never be."

"I feel you there. What now?"

He asks the million-dollar question that I haven't a clue how to answer. So I'm surprised when I say, "Take it as it comes. I'm gonna be honest and say I don't know if I want to run the show, but for now, we have obligations and a family the depends on us. But—I can't do this alone." I turn to him, saying earnestly, "I need you at my side as my right-hand. Both you and Jake. I'm not a one-man show like my father. If I do this, it will be the three of us all the way. That's the only way I'll even consider it." *And I know it's the absolute truth. We should have always been equals even though by blood we're not.*

He runs an unsteady hand through his hair, looking almost emotional.

I haven't stopped to consider how hard the news has been on the rest of my family. Everyone loved and revered my parents, and it decimates me to know that they will grieve them, grieve my mom, not knowing the truth. Not knowing she would have destroyed anyone she saw in the way of her malevolent goals. Not knowing how she attempted to murder my future. And that because of her, my father has been forcefully ejected from his throne. *His life.* But for everyone else, they will grieve people they believed in, trusted in, and people they will miss.

Pull it together, Moretti. Fuck. I look away, fighting for composure as well. He clears his throat, and I'm afraid he's going to say something sappy that'll have us both crying, but luckily, the real Nic comes out instead. "Oh, all right. Swear to fuck, dude, I'll help you out if you'll stop acting like such a little bitch." And for the first time since this awful nightmare happened, I finally laugh. And it's never felt so good.

EPILOGUE

Nina

I sit in the corner of the sofa with my arms wrapped around my knees and stare into space. It's pretty much how I've spent a good part of my time since being released from the hospital almost a month ago. I start each day determined to deal with what's happened, yet it never seems to get any further. Part of it is sheer exhaustion. Then there are the nightmares, the lack of sleep. My body is still trying to heal from the trauma of the gunshot and the surgery that followed. The doctor said it would take time and not to rush my recovery. And physically, other than fatigue, I am almost back to normal. I'm still short of breath at times, but considering the couch potato I've turned into, that's not surprising. Minka, as always, has been a lifeline. My friend, cheerleader, nurse, companion and the one who holds me at night when I wake up screaming. *The one who pretends not to notice when I cry —over him.*

She asked me last night why I wouldn't see him. Why I could forgive her for not being honest about her other life, yet not him. And I pointed out that she didn't kill my family, but he did. She said nothing further, because really, what could make it better?

If I were honest with myself, the inner struggle to accept what he did is what's wrecking me inside. I'm in love with him. And I want nothing more than to beg him to hold me and never let go. I truly fear I won't heal in my current state because my heart is shutting the rest of my body down. I'm grieving myself to death, and it has nothing to do with Franklin and everything to do with Marco.

When I regained consciousness in the hospital, he was the first face I saw. And for a moment, it had been everything. But then the ugly reality comes crashing in, and I became hysterical. If I close my eyes, I can still see the devastation on his handsome face as he held out a hand to me, silently pleading not to push him away. He'd needed me. After all, he had lost everything. Yet I had not been able to deal with what he'd done. I would have trusted him with my life. I believed in him, yet it felt as if I never really knew him at all. What I told Minka was true; I could have forgiven him for not telling me about the FBI, but he killed Franklin and Frankie. The entire time, he comforted me for a crime he committed. What kind of monster must that make him?

Even knowing that, why am I consumed with so much guilt where he's concerned? Why can't I get the look on his face that last time out of my mind? *I broke him.*

I'm still on the sofa, wallowing in self-pity, when Minka comes in an hour later. She moves to stand in front of me and puts her hands on her hips before releasing a long-suffering sigh. "This can't go on, Ni. You're killing not only him but yourself as well." I turn my head away as a tear escapes and rolls down my cheek. *Oh great, the waterworks are coming early tonight.* I'm surprised I have any tears left at this point. "I want you to remember that this is for your own good."

"I'm sorry." I sniffle, then freeze when her words get through. "Wh-what? Minka?" I shift, trying to see where she's gone, but there's nothing until the door slams a moment later. Apparently, she can't take it anymore. I guess this is one of those sink or swim moments. She's not going to stay with me anymore, and who can blame her? Even I don't want to be with me.

The tears are coming in earnest now. I'm so caught up in my misery that I scream when I hear, "Belle baby, don't."

My eyes jerk open, and there he is just inches away. The man who occupies all my waking and sleeping moments. My hell on earth. "Marco... how did you—"

He smiles faintly, putting his hands in his pockets and rocking back on his heels. It's a move I've noticed he does when he's nervous or unsure, and like most everything these days, it makes me want to cry. I pull the back of my hands across my damp face and self-consciously run a hand over my hair. I have no idea when I even washed it last. "Apparently, Minka and Nic are tired of our 'sad, fucking puppy-dog faces.' Nic told me you wanted me to come over tonight, then when I got here, Minka opened the door and spilled the beans that you didn't know. Then she pulled me in the door, shut it behind me, and left."

Unbelievably, I find myself smiling as well. "She's a little sick of dealing with me, I'm afraid. Wants me to get my act together."

"How are you? Minka says you're healing, but I've been so worried. Wondering if you were taking care of yourself. How you were handling —everything. Wishing you'd let me help you. Be here to hold you. I—"

"Stop," I whisper, my heart feeling as if it's shattering. His words are so stark and pain-filled that it's agony for me to even hear them. *Don't do this to me. Please, God, I can't take it.*

He's silent for a moment. I'm afraid he's going to leave, yet terrified he'll stay. Finally, he takes a seat on the coffee table in front of me. "Why can't you forgive me? I... I love you, Belle, and I know you love me. I see it in your eyes when you look at me. And being apart is killing both of us. Haven't we both suffered enough, baby?" *God, whenever I think of Marco, I get stuck on how much he has lost in this. What he now knows about his mother... his dad...* But I need answers.

"Why did you kill them? Just tell me that much. I realize I'm not even supposed to know about your other life, much less the fact that you killed my family. But why was it necessary?" I hold my hand out, not even sure what I'm asking for, and he takes it instantly between his own. *Feels so good. Hurts so fucking much.* "I—can even almost understand Frankie Jr. I know he was bad. Probably worse than I can imagine. But Franklin?"

He sighs, looking away for a moment, before turning back to me.

"Franklin was much more involved in his son's new business venture than anyone knew. Frankie was trafficking women. Had been doing it on a small scale for some time and keeping it hidden from the old man. But then he managed to lure in some partners, and things were getting big. He was pulling in some serious money and using one of our warehouses for part of it. We found out and confronted Franklin. He laughed it off. 'Boys will be boys.' We warned him that we would not allow it to continue. More than once. But he not only ignored the warnings, but he also invested a chunk of Gavino money in the operation and basically told us to mind our own fucking business. Yet he made it our business by using our property and probably our name. We were too closely linked with the Gavinos to allow something of that magnitude to happen. Not to mention the fact it's fucking sick. Those girls—fuck no." He pauses for a moment; the revulsion he feels evident. I don't think anything can surprise me at this point, yet his next words prove me wrong. "When Nic and I delivered his last warning, he let me know in no uncertain that he was fond of you and would hate it if you were to have an unfortunate accident." I look at him in disbelief. There's no way Franklin would have threatened me—*would he?*

Marco seems to be struggling with something, then he removes one hand from around mine and pulls his phone from his pocket. He taps a few keys and lays it on the table. My eyes widen when I hear Franklin's voice, along with Marco's. He left out a few things, but it's almost word for word what he just told me. Even though it's clearly Franklin's voice, the tone is completely different than I've ever heard before. There's a coldness that sounds too natural to be forced. Menacing. My first inclination would be to think he was bluffing Marco, thinking he'd back off to protect me. He even mentioned me disappearing in one of his shipment of girls as if he'd given it considerable thought. Before Angelica's betrayal, I would have likely needed more than this to convince me, but she changed something in me. *In all of us,* I think to myself, noting the dark circles under Marco's eyes. The bleakness he can't quite hide. *Pain. So much pain. He needs me, and God, do I need him.*

My bottom lip trembles violently. I can barely get the words out, but finally, I manage, "Wh-why didn't you?" That's as far as I get. He already knows what I'm asking at this point. Before he answers, he gets to his feet and leans down to scoop me into his arms. Then he stands there with his face buried in my neck, crushing me so tightly I'm afraid I'll snap. Yet it's the best pain I've ever felt. *He loves me enough to let me go. Completely selfless.*

After a while, he lowers himself to the sofa with me still clutched against him. "I didn't want to do that to you. To take away the man who'd been a father to you. After what my... mother did, I have no right to happiness if it meant taking yet another thing from you. I don't deserve you, I never have. You're good and pure. And I'm tainted by everything I've seen and done. I'll never be the man you need. One you'll be proud of, that—"

"Dear God"—I start laughing— "you absolutely suck at this, Moretti. Do you want to love me or make me end it all? That's the single most depressing speech I've heard since Minka's last self-help pitch."

He pulls back, staring at me in shock. *Look at that face. I hurt his feelings.* "And you think you could do better? You like chick books. I thought you'd appreciate a man pouring his heart out."

I roll my eyes, feeling strangely happy for someone who has just discovered their stepfather was an evil turd. *Maybe the apple hasn't fallen far from the tree after all.* "The men in my books are alpha-badasses, not pussies. They make their women happy in bed, not with sappy speeches. Maybe you should read one of them, then we'll try this again."

"Excuse me?" he chokes out, no doubt in disbelief that a woman would question the skills of the great Marco Moretti. I shake my head.

How could seeing him, being held by him, just breathing his scent somehow revive me?

Because he loves you enough to come even if he may have been rejected. I yawn and lean up to kiss his cheek. "I'm tired. Why don't you let yourself out, and we'll talk in a few days? Catch ya later, buddy."

About two seconds pass before I'm flat on my back with a growling man pushing one knee between my legs as he comes down over me. Even in his haste, his touch is gentle as if afraid I'll break. He stares at me as if seeing me for the first time all over again. "I love you, Belle. And I'm so sorry about—"

"I know. So am I." There is a time for laughter and a time for tenderness, and he needs the latter now. I cup the side of his face and smile when he turns into my touch. "I missed you so much. And I'm sorry you've had to go through this alone. I just didn't know how to handle everything." *His mother was going to kill me. I looked death in the eye.*

"You don't owe me an apology, baby. We've both suffered, and I know it's not going to be better overnight. I know you have questions. We still have a lot to talk about and to resolve, and I don't want any more secrets between us. We'll take everything slowly, just please... give me a chance, Belle. I can't lose you too."

"I'm not going anywhere," I vow as the final pieces of the past break away, and I see only the man before me. "I love you, Marco. I belong to you. I have for so very long." And finally, I'm where I need to be. We've fought through hell, yet we're still here. A tragedy and betrayal so significant that it should have broken us apart forever, yet we've found our way back to each other. I may not have been born mafia, but I was born to love this man. And the biggest blessing of all is that he was also born to love me.

Minka

Neither of them hears the door opening, nor the footsteps tiptoeing through my apartment to pause inches away. "Fuck me. Finally," Nic whispers as we glance at the sofa to see Nina and Marco sound asleep in each other's arms. They're holding each other so close, you can barely tell where one starts and the other stops.

I hold out a hand, and we fist-bump. "I figured they'd either kill or fuck each other to death."

Nic peers closer before asking, "Should we check them for breath? Make sure they picked door number two?"

Nina lets out a loud snore at precisely that moment, and we both stifle a laugh. "Yeah, I think they're good. Let's get out of here. I feel like a peeping pervert."

"That kind of turns me on," Nic mutters as he slides a hand down to pinch my ass. "I'd like you to demonstrate exactly how you'd go about the number two you speak of."

He continues groping me as we retrace our steps. When we reach the door, I pause for a moment, thinking something feels different. Then it hits me. The sorrow that's hung so heavily over all of us has temporarily subsided. Of course, it'll be back, but for tonight, our world is at peace, and I couldn't ask for anything more.

Except to know whether it's wisdom or stupidity to believe that there will never be retribution for the murders by my hands.

The End

Coming Fall 2019—Nicoli

ACKNOWLEDGMENTS

My amazing editors: Marion Archer and Jenny Sims with Editing4Indies. Love you, ladies!

Melissa Gill for my beautiful cover.

For my BFF Erik (Jethro) Real men read romance, right?

And to my friends, Elizabeth Swain, Shazza Fletcher, Sandy Ambrose, Sherri McJunkin, Katelyne Morgan, Jenni Lord with Between the Sheets Book Reviews, Catherine Crook with A Reader Lives a Thousand Lives, Jennifer Harried with Book Bitches Blog, Christine with Books and Beyond, Jenn with SMI Book Club, Chloe with Smart Mouth Smut, Shelly with Sexy Bibliophiles, Amanda and Heather with Crazy Cajun Book Addicts, Stacia with Three Girls & A Book Obsession, Lisa Salvary and Confessions of a Book Lovin Junkie.

THE PIERCED SERIES

Pierced

My name is Lucian Quinn and I own one of the most successful software companies in the world. I'm twenty-nine, rich and single. Impressive right? I'm also a favorite target for every hungry socialite looking to land the uncatchable catch. Maybe it sounds vain, but the fact that I'm a God between the sheets doesn't hurt my stock any. What these women don't know though is that I'm completely screwed up and damaged beyond repair by my past. The only part of me I'll ever willingly give them is the hour it takes to make them scream...several times.

Then I saw her...

Circumstances bring two people that should have never crossed paths together, and in the days and weeks ahead, they grow close quickly, each seeing a kindred soul in the other. As ghosts from their past rise to haunt them, they cling to each other as their lives start to spiral out of control. Soon, they realize that they're both damaged possibly beyond repair. Will their love be what saves or destroys them?

Fractured

Lucian and Lia attempt to deal with the aftermath of the violent attack on her by her stepfather. As events unfold in their lives, Lia finds that she can no longer be patient with the man that she loves, because his secrets are tearing them apart.

Lucian cannot deny the fact that he's fallen in love with the brave and beautiful woman who has lived a life of horror. He wants nothing more than to protect her, but soon realizes that he may be the person who will hurt her the most.

To be together, they'll have to fight demons from their pasts that threaten to destroy them.

Mended

Lucian finally shares his past heartache and guilt with Lia. Free of the shadows that have haunted them, they are ready to move forward together.

Until...the woman who destroyed Lucian's life eight years ago is suddenly free. Lucian is in a frantic race against time to convince those around him that Cassie is the ultimate threat to all that he holds dear. He'll stop at nothing to protect the woman he loves even if he must wage a war against his best friend to do it.

Rose

My name is Rose Madden and I have spent my life being the perfect daughter. Thanks to my daddy, I'm an expert marksman who dresses like some modern-day freaking June Cleaver. My life has been perfectly scripted since the day I was born. I've never deviated from the plan—until I met attorney Max Decker. Now he has me doing insane things to get his attention, like grabbing him in his car and being arrested for stalking my ex-boyfriend just so he'll come bail me out of jail. He thinks

I'm crazy—but he wants me anyway. Will he still feel the same when fate steps in, revealing my secret shame to him?

Aidan

"She's a dirty-talking, sassy-mouthed handful who keeps me on my toes. I never know what's going to come out of that mouth next, and it turns me on like you wouldn't believe."

Aidan Spencer walked away from his family and his friends when the woman he'd loved since childhood died while attempting to kill his best friends' wife. Aidan had chosen to save another and in doing so had lost Cassie. For over a year, he's been isolated from everyone he loves until a family emergency brings him back home. When he meets a woman along the way whose problems are direr than his own, he must decide if he's strong enough to fight for the woman he's falling in love with knowing there's no promise of a tomorrow for them?

Lee

My name is Lee Jacks and I've lived a life that few could imagine. When you grow up as the son of a crack whore with little more than the clothes on your back most days being accepted by your peers is the last thing you expect. I was always an outcast which was fine by me. It's what kept my brother and me alive. Survival is something that isn't taught in public schools, but it damn well should be. Especially the one that I attended for a while. But I'm no longer a gutter rat to be kicked aside like yesterday's trash. I'm a sought-after member of the Asheville, North Carolina elite and invited to parties given by the mayor, governor and the upper crust of society.

If there's one thing I've learned, money and power will turn many an eye blind and even more ears deaf. Rumors about my past and the fact that I've long operated in the grey areas of the law abound, but the good people in this city could give a f***. What they do care about is that I donate to whatever charity their guilty conscience prods them to support.

Even as a kid I instinctively knew that I needed to be the alpha. That's the same ingrained knowledge that animals are born with. You assert your dominance early on and reinforce it as needed. It wasn't that I enjoyed fighting as some did. Hell, I'd never considered myself a violent man by nature. But if it comes down to the him or me scenario, then it's gonna be him every time. I've killed to protect myself and those I love and I wouldn't hesitate to do it again.

The one thing I never counted on was falling in love with my assistant Liza. In one of my few selfless acts, I refused to bring her into my corrupt world. When she quits her job, and walks away from me, I soon discover that I never really knew her at all. For she has secrets of her own and one of them could very well be the need to destroy me.

Anthony

My name is Anthony Moretti and I'm the prince of the Moretti family. Although I'm not active in the crime syndicate that my father, Draco Moretti, began, I'll always be protected by the family and feared by those outside of it.

After my father was gunned down in the street, I used my inheritance from him to open my first nightclub. For years, building my empire was my only concern, until fate brought Jacey Wrenn into my life. She had absolutely no idea, but I'd known her before I'd ever met her. She'd haunted my dreams, the beautiful stranger that I longed to find, but hadn't a clue as to where to begin.

Sounds like a fairy tale, right? I wish. The woman that I've been obsessed with for years is broken so badly, I'm not sure if I can save her. Hell, how does the son of the devil convince a fallen angel that redemption is possible for people like us?

Marco

My name is Marco Moretti and I'm the son of the Moretti Crime Family boss. He's also my father and a bit of an asshole, but we all have problems, don't we? I've always loved women of all shapes and sizes and they've loved me in return. Sometimes a bit too much, but a stalker or two keeps things interesting. My position within "the family" has been the most important thing to me, until fate—and food poisoning brought Nina Gavino into my life. I've finally found the woman that I can't live without, and she wants nothing to do with me. My usual charm has gotten me nowhere. And if she ever finds out that I killed her stepfather and stepbrother, I'm afraid nothing short of a miracle, will make the beautiful spitfire, give me a chance to prove that there is more to me than the job she holds so much contempt for.

Nicoli

I lean my hip against the second-floor balcony and glare at the dark-haired woman below. "What in the fuck is she doing?" I snap to my club manager, Jax Hudson.

Jax shrugs his shoulders indifferently. "Don't know for sure, boss. Seems like a weird place to hold a job interview, but that's what it looks like. She's got people filling out paperwork, and hell, there's even a pen stuck in her hair. She's hot, though, so maybe I should go apply for whatever this position is. I've always had a thing for the nerdy accountant look. Shit, look, she's wearing glasses with those granny neck straps." He licks his lips in a way that makes me want to punch his face. "That's smoking."

Rolling my eyes, I shake my head in resignation. If I've learned nothing else in my time as owner of one of the hottest clubs in town, it's that people are basically nuts. I'm not surprised anymore, but seeing the woman below in a pale silk blouse collecting papers from the group of men who surround her table is a first. Even from a distance, something about her is vaguely familiar. Her slim build and the curve of her neck stir something in my conscience, but I can't place what it is. Even my body is reacting to her, which is downright insane. I'm surrounded by scantily dressed women every night—most of whom throw themselves at me regularly. So why in the fuck would I look twice at some uptight broad who's obviously picked a bad place to conduct whatever business she has. "Go down and see what's going on. Her little enterprise is blocking the entrance to the bar."

Jax straightens away from the banister saying, "You got it, boss," before leaving to do my bidding.

I remain where I am out of curiosity as he reaches the bottom floor and approaches the table in question. He weaves his through the group of men and leans down to speak in the woman's ear. She nods a few times, then looks up. Her eyes search the area before locking on mine, and I hiss in shock. *Holy fucking shit.*

Jacey. The hair is different, but I know the face. It's haunted my dreams for months.

Coming Fall 2019

ALSO BY SYDNEY LANDON

THE DANVERS NOVELS

Weekends Required

Not Planning on You

Fall For Me

Fighting For You

No Denying You

Always Loving You

Watch Over Me

The One For Me

Wishing For Us

THE BREAKFAST IN BED SERIES

Keeping it Hot

Room For Two

THE PIERCED SERIES

Pierced

Fractured

Mended

Rose

Aidan

Lee

Anthony

Marco

Nicoli (Fall 2019)

ABOUT THE AUTHOR

Sydney Landon is the New York Times & USA Today Best Selling author of: Weekends Required, Not Planning on You, Fall For Me, Fighting For You, Betting on You, No Denying You, Always Loving You, Pierced and Fractured. Sydney is currently working on the next book in the Danvers' Series as well as the Pierced Series. When she isn't writing, Sydney enjoys reading, swimming and the beach. She lives with her family in Greenville, South Carolina.

Represented by:
Jane Dystel, Dystel & Goderich Literary Management, Union Square West, Suite 904, New York, NY 10003, (212)627-9100 ext. 12

www.sydneylandon.com
sydneylandon36@yahoo.com

BB bookbub.com/authors/sydney-landon

f facebook.com/sydney.landonauthor

instagram.com/sydneylandon36

twitter.com/SydneyLandon1

pinterest.com/slandon36

Nicoli (Fall 2019)

Lucian & Lia Trilogy

Made in the USA
Middletown, DE
17 December 2019

81030621R00113